ROGUE

The Genesis Files, Book 1

BONNIE SYNCLAIRE

Synclaire Books

Copyright © 2018 by Bonnie Synclaire

All rights reserved. Published by Synclaire Publishing and Lulu.com. No portion of this book may be reproduced or transmitted in any form or by any means, electronic or mechanical, including photocopying, recording, or by any information storage and retrieval system, without permission from the publisher.

This is a work of fiction. Names, characters, places, and incidents either are the products of the author's imagination or are used fictitiously. Any resemblance to actual persons, living or dead, businesses, companies, events, or locales is entirely coincidental.

First Edition, April 2018

Printed in the United States of America
This book is set in 12 point Garamond
Cover image from www.pexels.com under Creative Commons Zero (CC0)
Cover design by Bonnie Synclaire

Summary: "Identical twins Harper and Joanna quickly learn about their father's dark past that's linked to an underground organization after their parents' sudden disappearance, and realize that their lives are in danger."—Provided by publisher.
Identifiers: ISBN 978-1-387-70772-0
Subjects: | Sisters, Twins—Fiction. | Organizations—Fiction. | Orphans—Fiction. | FBI Projects—Fiction.

Visit the author's website:
www.bonniesynclaire.com

"Captivating, gripping, and dynamic...*Rogue* is an intriguing story highlighting the unbreakable bond between two sisters. With hearts being torn when they think their parents have turned on them makes for rising tensions and a suspense-filled journey through dangerous circumstances. Culminating with a cliffhanger ending that foreshadows peace and solace may be much farther away than they hope. This leaves us on the edge of our seat wanting more to see the next steps these sisters will have to endure in finding out the truth that will finally set them free."

- Kerri M.

"*Rogue* is a riveting, fast-paced thriller that takes you into the shadowy world of spy agencies and criminal enterprises. You'll immediately connect with Harper and Jo, rooting for the twins through shocking twists and turns. Agent-in-training Skye and mysterious D help the twins uncover their parents' true identities, revealing secrets of their own along the way. Rich in detail, with a narrative that evokes both suspense and empathy, this book is a must-read that will leave you eagerly anticipating a sequel."

- Kristen R.

For Grandma Bonnie.
I wish you could hold this.

And for my family.

- B.S.

Author's Note to Readers:
Acre Wood is a fictional town.
All other locations are real.

1

FRIDAY, DECEMBER 15, 2017
2:11 P.M.
MONTPELLIER ACADEMY

Harper

THE BEGINNING, FOR ME anyway, starts with a letter:

Harper,

You don't know who I am, and I don't think you ever will, so don't try to find me. I just thought I should give you a heads-up.

I haven't forgotten about your father—the traitor to me, to our fellow Brothers, to even you, your sister, and your mother. You may think you know who he is, but you don't know his true identity. I suppose you'll find that out soon enough.

Now he is in danger, and so are you and your family. His past has come back to haunt him, and now there's no running from all the wrongs he'd committed over a decade ago. I can't tell you much right now, but I can tell you one thing: don't trust anyone after you read this. Also, don't tell anyone about this letter. If you do, I can't guarantee your life. Nor my own.

- D

It's on a wrinkled piece of yellow paper, slipped inside my locker at school.

I don't notice it until after the school day, as I'm stuffing things into my backpack to take home for winter break. At first I simply ignore it. I fold the paper up several times before shoving it into my backpack and leaving the building, but the tense feeling that I'm being watched grows with each step I take. I try to convince myself that this is just a silly prank, but a nagging feeling in my chest tells me that something isn't quite right.

I meet Joanna, my twin sister, outside the main building of our school, Montpellier Academy. Most people call her Jo. We get on our assigned bus and sit in the seat that's right behind the driver's. I wrap my scarf tighter around my neck, stomp at the ground to get the sticky slush off my boots, twist my curls with my fingers, unbutton my coat then button it back up again so the loops are even. My sister watches me closely—I swear she's a mind-reader. Or, maybe it's just obvious that something's on my mind.

'You OK?' she signs. I nod. I'll decide whether or not I want to tell her about the letter when we get home, when we'll be alone, and hopefully later with our parents when they get home from work.

Our parents work for Genesis, our grandfather's spy agency in the city. It's hidden in plain sight behind massive skyscrapers and buildings—not even the President knows Granddad's agency exists, let alone it's one of the top agencies in North America. Mom is an undercover cop, and she teaches coding classes at our school in the mornings. Jo and I have no idea what our father does, though. He always comes home at midnight, but I don't know if I can wait that long to tell him about the letter I just found in my locker. The bus lurches forward.

Ten minutes later, we arrive in Winchester, the neighborhood in Acre Wood that Jo and I live in. Winchester is mostly made up of unclaimed land—dozens of acres as far as the eye can see—with centuries-old family farms accompanied by their ritzy family estates here and there. We live in a house on Verdure Avenue's cul-de-sac, accompanied by two acres of flat, too-green grass behind it. But we don't have a family farm or anything.

The school bus stops at the intersection of Verdure Avenue and Manor Road, and Jo and I get off. I see our house in the distance, a five-bedroom, red brick, Acadian-style house with a faded black roof, ugly beige shutters that Dad won't replace, and dying landscaping due to the bitter Pennsylvania winters. We walk to the garage keypad and I punch in the code, *4-8-9-1*, the year our parents were born typed backward. One garage door opens with a lazy tug and squeak, and we step inside. Our parents' cars are here, Dad's shiny black Lincoln and Mom's older red Jeep, which to me is odd; they're never home this early, ever.

The whole house is cold and dark. The aching feeling in my chest quickly returns, stronger now. It's like a sixth sense that I've had since I was little. Jo doesn't seem to notice or even care as she goes into the kitchen. Mom and Dad haven't responded to any of my texts all day too, I remember.

I go upstairs to my bedroom and lock the door behind me. I take the letter out of my backpack, close all the curtains, and turn on the lamp on my nightstand. I sit down on my queen size bed, unfold the letter, and read it again. *I haven't forgotten about your father…traitor…true identity…in danger…can't guarantee your life…nor my own…*This has to be some kind of joke. Dad can make sense of all this. At least, he'd better.

* * *

I spend the evening in the den with Jo, watching Christmas movie marathons and guzzling root beer. We don't really do a lot during holidays; Mom's half sisters always claim they're busy, and Jo and I don't know a thing about Dad's family, and no one ever offers to tell us.

"Hey. Hey. Jo." It's 7:30, and Jo is dozing off on my shoulder. We're sitting on the brown leather theater couch, the end credits of *The Nightmare Before Christmas* on the 52-inch TV. I poke her shoulder. She glares, adjusting her hearing aid on her right ear. I notice her ears are a deep red.

"Wanna order a pizza?" I ask. She shakes her head. "McDonald's?" Shakes her head again. "Golden Lantern?" She gives a short shrug. If Jo would have turned down Golden Lantern, the best Chinese food place in town, I don't know what I would have done. She's stubborn and picky, just like Mom. I eat anything that's handed to me, just like Dad.

Dad…

"Jo," I say again. I have to tell her about the letter now; it's been in the back of my mind ever since I'd discovered it in my locker. How did it get on our school's campus anyway?

Jo breathes out through her flaring nose and sits up to face me, obviously annoyed that I won't let her doze off in peace, but I could care less right now. I take the letter out of the red and black letterman jacket I'm wearing and hand it to her. "This was in my locker. I have no idea where it came from."

Jo turns the volume down on the TV and reads the paper. Her eyes widen, and I think she rereads it a few times. Instead of speaking, she decides to sign to me. Jo does that sometimes. 'Handwriting' she signs.

"I don't know anyone with that handwriting." I say.

'Who's D?' Jo signs, then points to the single letter hastily scribbled at the bottom of the paper.

I shrug. "Who do we know whose name starts with D?"

'Deedee, Dewey, and Dre.' Jo signs each letter of her response with the fingers of her dominant hand, which is her right hand, spelling out each name.

I know Deedee. She's one of Jo's only friends and has the same exact schedule as her; she knows sign language because her little brother is deaf, so she helps Jo in school a lot. Montpellier is strict on bringing people on and off campus, but Mom has been trying to persuade the principal to hire a real aid for a while. But for now, Deedee seems to work. To Jo, Deedee is short for Diana Sanders. She's on Montpellier Academy's varsity cheerleading team, vice-president of the ASL club, and the sophomore student government treasurer. Jo is only deaf in her right ear and hard-of-hearing in the other.

Dewey and Dre Johnson are identical twin boys at our school. They're juniors and Jo and I are sophomores. We're good friends. We used to hang out all the time when we were little; Dewey and Dre's mom is a cop, just like our mom, and they worked together a lot. Jo and I also went to the town's Harvest dance with them last year.

"None of those people would send a note like this, none of them are stupid enough to play a trick on us." I say, matter-of-factly. "Should we tell Mom and Dad? Should we call Genesis, or the police?" Jo shrugs, taking her hearing aids off and curling up at my side, linking her arm with mine. She doesn't want to deal with my paranoia today. I sigh, stuffing the letter back into my pocket, not bothering folding it back into tiny squares again.

* * *

I think we fell asleep, because when I wake up, it's eleven o'clock and Jo is fast asleep, still curled up at my side. I retrieve my cell phone from the pocket opposite of the letter and turn it on. A migraine tugs at the backs of my eyes, hunger gnaws at my stomach. There are no unread texts or missed calls from Mom or Dad. I look at the time again just to make sure I'm not hallucinating. 11:52 p.m.

I stand and stretch out my sore limbs, careful not to wake my sister as I lay her down on the couch and put my letterman jacket over her. I turn off the TV and head upstairs. Goosebumps cover my skin as I walk through the living room and into the kitchen. I'd taken off my school uniform earlier and put it in the washer machine, my thin underclothes aren't a big help in the cold rooms of the house. The whole house is still dark, cold, silent—just not right.

I scavenge the kitchen for something to eat, but there's not much here. So I decide to head down to the garage. I open the door and peer inside. It's dark in here too. Dad's Lincoln and Mom's Jeep are still here, but my parents are nowhere to be seen. Where are they?

I head back down to the den. "Hey. Jo." I say, kneeling down beside her and shaking her shoulder gently. She doesn't budge, but she's a deep sleeper, so I don't think much of it. "Hey, Jo." Still no answer. Beads of sweat coat her forehead, her breathing faint and shallow. I glance at the thermostat on the wall. The number 57 stares back at me. That's weird. It's cold in here and Jo is sweating terribly. I press the back of my hand to her forehead and wait. She's burning up.

I put my letterman jacket back on and try to wake Jo up. I shake her shoulders, say her name over and over, but none of it does any good. I keep going though for a minute or two before Jo finally fidgets. Then she starts to cough. I rub her back and hit it a few times to help her. By the way her lungs sound, they're diminished. Jo coughs some more raspy coughs. When Jo suddenly gets sick like this, she needs to be hospitalized. Without Mom or Dad here, we can't go anywhere; we're too young to drive. We're stuck in the house. I could call for an ambulance, but I don't want to draw any attention to ourselves, especially when I still have no idea about where the creepy letter came from.

All I can do now is care for Jo by myself, and hope Mom and Dad will come home soon.

2

FRIDAY, DECEMBER 15, 2017
12:15 P.M.
GENESIS HQ

Skye

"NINE," A VOICE CALLS, and I stop in my tracks. "Number Nine, where do you think you're going?"

I sigh, letting the glass door close with a soft *click*. I turn to face my boss, chin up, shoulders back, posture square. "I-I finished my morning training," I tell her, trying to keep my tone even, though I can't hide the slight tremor in my voice. "I-I'm on my noon-to-two break."

"Well, you're not getting a break today; the new trainees need settling in, and you and the other oldest trainees are going to help them. And you know you can't leave headquarters anyway. You're really lucky I never tell Mr. Cambridge about your escape attempts." Ms. McCoy says, crossing her arms. I want to protest but I know I can't, she basically owns me.

Ever since I've stepped foot inside Genesis, my name has been 9. I and nine other orphans are training to become undercover cops, spies, assassins, or special agents. I'm going to be a member of the FBI or CIA when I turn eighteen, but it's nowhere near as glamorous as it sounds.

Every few years or so, Genesis secretly goes to a remote orphanage in Cape May, New Jersey, which is about five hours away from here, and takes ten children to be in the Elite Training Program. They give us numbers, not names, and nobody knows we exist. When we graduate from the ETP when we're eighteen, we are given a real name for agents and officials to call you by, and if you get to go on a mission you get your own code names. Sometimes you get your real name early. Last time I checked, my name is Skye.

Nevertheless, none of us will ever truly exist—we either die during our first mission or are always undercover.

Now, Ms. McCoy walks to where I'm standing and drops a thick manila folder into my hands. "Pass these out to the new trainees and give a tour of headquarters. Everyone is waiting in the residence wing." And at that she walks away, her shiny black stilettos clicking along the sparkling gray granite floors, the floors I clean every over day. I groan and head back down the hall.

* * *

Ms. McCoy was the one who picked me.

I remember sitting in my room at Brades Orphanage at age eleven, teaching one of my roommates how to unlock a computer without putting in the password, when the door opened, and she was standing there with Sister Clarence. The orphanage was supposed to be a religious one, but I'd never witnessed anything religious about Brades. I startled, and the old computer I'd stolen from the janitor's closet fell to the ground with a loud *crash*, and a few buttons popped off. I wasn't a bad kid, but I was sneaky at times. I was just bored, and fascinated by technology. Maybe Sister Clarence knew what I'd been doing all along, and when McCoy came for her usual cloak-and-dagger business, she had told them about me.

My roommate scurried away before Sister Clarence could close the door. "Delilah," she said sternly. That was what my mother named me, Delilah, before she'd abandoned me when I was two. At least, that's what it says on my paperwork.

I didn't look at Sister Clarence, who cleared her throat and stood up straight. She was a soft spoken, twenty-something year old nun, but she took charge when she needed to. "I'd like to introduce you to Ms. Erin McCoy. She's here to recruit ten new children to participate in her training program." It was obvious that Sister Clarence barely knew anything about McCoy or Genesis, but eleven-year-old me didn't catch her oblivion then.

I looked up at Erin McCoy. Even four years ago she looked the same. Her hair was long and jet-black, pulled into a perfect low bun, had tight pale skin with no wrinkles or falters at all, piercing dark brown eyes behind her black circular glasses. She was five-foot-eight, her heels made her look like a giant.

I stood from the creaky wooden bunk bed. I wore a used yellow dress and white socks, no shoes. My raven-black hair was untamed, my blue eyes sparkling with curiosity. My face was round and covered in freckles, not yet changing like everyone else's, though my body was bony and pale.

"Delilah…" Ms. McCoy said my name as if it were a foreign language, but I beamed. "Sister Clarence told me about your knack of getting into things you're not supposed to." She glanced at the computer beside my feet, and I felt my cheeks burn red with embarrassment. "I am Ms. Erin McCoy, the new president of the elite child training program at a project created by the FBI."

"Okay." I said shyly, not really understanding.

Ms. McCoy didn't seem to hear me, or now that I think about it, she probably just ignored me. She sighed. "Congratulations. You have been chosen to train with me. Please come with me. Everything will be explained later." She said everything, including the congratulations, in monotone.

I blinked, trying to process everything she just said. *Child training program…FBI…Congrats.* I didn't understand. What eleven-year-old would?

"Is she adopting me?" I whispered to Sister Clarence as she opened the door for Ms. Erin McCoy.

Ms. McCoy scoffed. "Not even close. I hate kids."

* * *

I didn't get a chance to say goodbye to anyone. I followed Ms. McCoy down the long redwood halls and outside, still without shoes. A black van awaited us, and I stopped in my tracks. I knew vans like that were dangerous, ones with no windows or license plates. What if this was a trick? What if—?

Ms. McCoy groaned and urged me toward the van. Two men in black suits and sunglasses guarded the perimeter of the van, and nodded stiffly when they saw Ms. McCoy. One of them opened the van door. I hesitated, but stepped inside. Nine other orphans I vaguely recognized were here too, fastened in and waiting. There was one seat left, beside my best friend Zed. He was twelve then, I was eleven.

I cautiously sat in the oddly comfortable seat and fastened the seat belt. "Zed, what's going on?" I whispered, but he just shrugged. I was shocked; Zed knew everything.

I didn't know the other orphans by name, but I did know Claude and James. Zed knew them too. They always picked on me and stole my food.

The van roared to life, and we began our drive to the unknown destination. The middle and back windows were boarded up, but I could see past the driver's seat and through the large front window. Ms. McCoy and the two men I saw just seconds ago sat on the floor, looking through papers and talking in low voices. A few minutes later I caught a glimpse of a sign: *Philadelphia - 93 mi.*

"Alright." one of the men said, turning to face us. The other man and Ms. McCoy continued to read. "Do any of you know what's happening?" We all shook our heads, silent. "The ten of you are the newest editions to Genesis's Elite Training Program. This is your new life now."

"So, this is, like, the FBI or something?" Claude asked.

"Genesis was created by the FBI, yes." the man said. "From here on out, you will train to become an undercover cop, special agent, spy, or assassin. On your eighteenth birthdays, you will receive your earned titles and begin working for us, with a new public name and multiple code names. You will not leave headquarters until you have received your title. If you try to leave, or if you purposefully break one of the rules or threaten Genesis or the FBI in any way…the new protocol is to either kill you or banish you. No one can find out about Genesis's new way of running things. *No one.*"

A few orphans gasped or fidgeted in their seats. "And why not, Mr. FBI?" Claude said. I could feel my muscles tense; I had a feeling he wouldn't last long in his "new life."

The man glared. "Because the new program hasn't been legalized."

* * *

Now, as my memory ends, I watch Ms. McCoy leave. The manila file folder is heavy in my arms, overflowing with papers. I take it to the residence wing of headquarters, where the rec room door is propped open.

Here are the nine people I came here with four years ago, including Zed, who has noticeably grown older, talking with the new young trainees. They all look excited. I remember the day I'd first arrived at Genesis. I was scared, lonely, and just plain confused. Ms. McCoy scared me then. Only Zed stayed by my side all these years, while the others simply kept their distance from me. Perhaps because I was the only one out of our group training to become an assassin, and I was getting the most hurt out of all of us during training.

Zed walks up to me, wraps a firm arm around my shoulder, and kisses my temple. "Hey. You okay?" he asks. He takes the folder from me and opens it, immediately going over the new trainees' information from Brades.

"Yeah." I mutter. "Let's just get this over with."

3

SATURDAY, DECEMBER 16, 2017
12:02 A.M.
CAMBRIDGE ESTATE

Harper

IT'S MIDNIGHT WHEN I help Jo up to my bedroom, and she instantly falls asleep in my bed, exhausted.

I lock every door and window in the house, close all the curtains, turn some lights on and off, set the thermostat to 72, turn off all the Christmas lights and the tree and the decorations, before collapsing beside Jo. I sent out at least a dozen texts and a few voicemails to both Mom and Dad's work phones and cell phones in the process, and they still haven't gotten back to me.

* * *

I awake to bright sunlight piercing through the window curtains and on my face. Still paranoid and grumpy, I sit up groggily and look at the digital clock on my nightstand. 9:33 a.m.

I silently slip into my letterman jacket, grab my iPhone from its charger, and head downstairs to the kitchen. On my way there, I stop at my parents' bedroom and open the door. The light is off. They're not there.

In the kitchen, I make myself and Jo two mugs of hot chocolate, then sit in the sunroom that overlooks the two acres of land. It must have snowed late last night; there's at least a foot of fluffy white snow on the ground, more falling from the pink and blue pastel sky. I sigh as I take a sip of my drink and scroll through my phone. No texts, calls, emails. Nothing. So I decide to call

Aunt Veronica. Mom's name is Victoria, and she has three older half sisters: Veronica, Vivienne, and Valentina, but only Mom and Aunt Veronica live here in Acre Wood. Aunt Veronica is the only one who is ever nice to Mom, and she's the only one who bothers to put herself into my and Jo's lives. I know her phone number by heart. She picks up on the first ring.

"Harper?" her voice says on the other end of the line.

"Hey, Aunt V. Are you busy?" I say.

"Not right now. How are you doing? Is school good? You're not getting into any trouble, are you?"

"Everything's good…Can I ask you something, though?"

"Of course. What's wrong?" Aunt Veronica questions.

"Well, it's Mom and Dad. Something's wrong but I don't know what. I've been trying to reach them since yesterday, and they still haven't gotten back to me. Do you know what's going on?"

I hear Aunt Veronica sigh into the phone. "I don't know about your father, but your mother texted me last night saying not to come over for the holidays, that there's been a change of plans. There's nothing too major going on at work, so I wonder what she meant." I furrow my eyebrows together in confusion, even though I know Aunt V can't see me. Mom has invited her over for just about every holiday since before I was born, but I'm not too worried about Dad; no one ever knows about him. I don't know what he does at work, what his family is like or anything.

"Why would she say that? Did she call or text you at all after that?"

"No, she hasn't. Isn't she home by now? Where's Joanna?"

"She's—" I start, but the sound of a single gunshot suddenly rips through the other end of the line, followed by a scream and muffled voices and shuffling feet. My chest tightens, my blood runs cold.

"A-Aunt V?" I stammer, not quite processing what's happening. "Aunt V, what happened? Hello?" No response. The sound of heavy feet shuffling around is the only sound that's left, and the line goes dead.

* * *

I let my cell phone fall onto my lap as I try to think about what just happened, the screen still on Aunt Veronica's contact picture, my body frozen in shock. Did someone break into her house or something? Did I hear a gun? Is she *alive*?

I put my phone in my pocket and abandon my hot chocolate as I race to my bedroom. Jo is still sound asleep. Just as I'm about to wake her up to tell her what happened, the doorbell rings. I head into the foyer, confused; the doorbell is rarely used. I open the front door without thinking, and something stops me right in my tracks.

A yellow notebook is taped to the ground.

My hands tremble as I hurry to rip it up off the ground. I blink a few times as I look around, searching for anything or anyone that could be out of place. Then I see. A tall figure in all black and coated in fresh snowflakes is walking down the driveway. They take one step onto Verdure Avenue, their large hood covering their face. "Hey!" I call out, my voice hoarse, and the figure halts. They turn to face me, and I can see about half of their face. It seems to be an older man. Pale skin, groomed moustache, a pink scar running along the lower side of his face. He walks backward until he's standing in the middle of the cul-de-sac, then pulls out something small and black. My breath catches in my throat. At first I think it's a gun, but it's just his phone. He types, and my own phone buzzes in my pocket. Stunned, I take it out and look down at the notification. It's a text. From him.

Him: Sorry I couldn't warn you sooner, you know, about Veronica. Don't worry, she's alive.

My eyes not leaving him for a second, I blindly text back, my heart pounding in my ears.

Me: Who are you?

Him: I'm the one writing to you.

Me: ???

Him: I'm the good guy here. Just remember that.

And at that, he shoves his phone back into his pocket, and he begins to sprint. He runs so fast that in just a few moments, he's out of sight.

I swear under my breath as I close the front door and lock it, then sit down in the dining room. My mind is racing, and I can't seem to pull myself together as I shakily lay the notebook down on the table and open to the first page. I read:

Harper,

I hope you realize that you are in danger. As of my identity…you'll find out soon enough. Maybe in my next letter, if our situation is where it needs to be. Just call me D. Communication-wise, we may communicate through text only, with "Unknown Number" as my name; my phone number changes a lot for identity purposes.

Now for a little history lesson. Our first topic: Scorpion. They're the reason for all of this.

There's an illegal organization located right in this city. They adapted the name Scorpion. Your father, Martin, and I became official members when we were sixteen. At first, the organization was like a haven to him, to all of us Brothers—they had money, loyalty, power on the streets, respect intertwined with fear. While we worked for them, they supplied us with thousands of dollars of illegally-printed money, jewelry, expensive clothing. But soon your father met your mother, and he immediately changed, and the whole haven illusion quickly faded.

Scorpion was actually a spy agency project created by the FBI, specializing in turning young people into spies, assassins, special agents, undercover cops. But things started going wrong, and the agents were scarred by the one event that caused them to rebel, turning into an underground organization out for revenge on the man who made the program, along with the people linked to him. I am one of the members who is still haunted by the Scorpion Project to this day. But your father has nothing to do with the Scorpion Project; he joined the illegal alteration just because.

The man who created Scorpion was your grandfather, Ronaldo Cambridge. He has an impressive FBI title, and was given a grant to start his own spy agency project. But he apparently wasn't good enough to hold a president position in such a business, and after he shut down Scorpion and basically kicked me and the other agents to the curb with nothing but the clothes on our backs (we didn't have names or any form of identity either), he wanted to try again. And the Genesis Project was born.

You already know your mother Victoria is an undercover cop for Genesis. She was on an assignment to spy on the now illegal and underground Scorpion and give information about our next trade meeting to your grandfather, and Martin had caught her. If he was any other member of the underground Scorpion, Martin would've simply dragged her to Boss's office and have her killed on the spot. But he didn't. Martin made a deal with Victoria to keep their encountering a secret.

About a month later at Scorpion HQ, he'd gushed to me about her for hours. But Victoria made one of her many mistakes: she let a target from her mission get too close to her, and their connection risked everything, for both us and Genesis. However, Martin was determined to prove to Victoria that he wasn't who underground Scorpion cut him out to be. But she was too dangerous for Martin—for all of the Brothers of Scorpion; she could easily snitch to her father and have the remainders of the Scorpion Project terminated for good.

How do I know so much about your father? you ask. Because we were best friends.

When we were eighteen, Martin's life changed forever. Victoria was pregnant (with you and your twin sister). Our roles in underground Scorpion were becoming more dangerous, and more deadly; at that time, Scorpion was nearly finished plotting their mission to destroy the Genesis Project. The mission to destroy Genesis is called Operation Zero. Underground Scorpion finished their plotting and started Phase 1 when you and your sister were six, but it failed. The next full attempt is in two weeks, on the night of December 30...

Scorpion wants Genesis's resources and knowledge, so we can expand our underground empire and turn our name into something bigger, so we can gain more power, money, weapons, underground allies. This will charge up our underground markets, and make us more respected, and feared, by more towns than just Acre Wood. To add fuel to the fire, Martin betrayed us and went to work for the Genesis Project with Victoria and

Ronaldo, shortly after he learned Victoria was having twins. He chose to train to become a freelance assassin, and after just months of training he was given his first mission: terminate the rest of the Scorpion Project.

By the time Martin found out about Operation Zero, it was too late. He loved Victoria once upon a time, yes, but the two of them and later you and your sister were trapped. It seemed Martin had finally realized he was too smart for underground Scorpion, but it was too late to change; after becoming a member and getting the official code tattoo when he was sixteen, he'd dropped out of high school. He knew Victoria and her babies weren't safe, so that's why Victoria's father offered him a job at Genesis, and soon after, was able to take all of you off the grid. Victoria and Martin vowed to protect you and your sister at any cost, even though they no longer wanted to protect each other.

So why am I telling you all this? You needed to know your parents' real backstory. You also needed to know what Genesis really is, and how it originated. The less you know, the more in danger you are. And you may end up like Veronica...

I have to stop writing now, but don't worry, we'll continue our history lesson very soon.

- D

* * *

I slump down in my chair and hold my head in my hands. This can't be happening. This isn't real. This is a game. That's it. A cruel game.

But it's not.

I text D, concentrating on keeping my shaky hands still: How did you get my number?

Connections, is his response two minutes later.

I purse my lips and fidget in my chair, automatically annoyed. Is he serious? I text back: Where are my parents & my aunt?

D: To be honest, I don't know yet. But when I find out, you have to promise not to tell anyone about anything. I will tell you everything at the right time.

Me: What about the police? Can't they help?

D: You can, but the police force won't do us any good; there are 2 crooked cops right here in Acre Wood working for Scorpion: John Earl & Antoine Gold. If they come to your house, do not let them in. If you cannot identify them, just be careful. Any other policemen are safe to talk to—at least, I hope. Do you swear you won't tell anyone about me?

I hesitate. This is obviously real. I obviously need help.
    But I do not text back.

4

SATURDAY, DECEMBER 16, 2017
6:30 P.M.
GENESIS HQ

Skye

THAT EVENING, WE TAKE the new trainees to the dining hall for dinner. Tonight's special is ribs with potato patch fries, mashed potatoes, and salad. But the inside of the ribs are pink, the fries are cold, and the chefs didn't bother giving us anything to decorate our salads with, not even ranch dressing.

I sit down next to Zed at one of the long oakwood tables and give him my tray of food. The new trainees are talking amongst themselves, practically buzzing with excitement. There are five boys and five girls, all the age of twelve. In my and Zed's group there are three girls and seven boys, and we were all in between eleven and thirteen when we came here. The other two girls haven't said more than three words to me since we were taken. Everyone talks to Zed, though.

"Why aren't you eating?" Zed asks, his mouth stuffed with mashed potatoes.

"Not hungry." I mutter.

"You're not still upset about this whole thing, are you? It's been *four years*. Aren't you happy you're out of Brades?"

"I guess," I reply. "But, remember what that guy said when we were in that van that day? He said this program isn't even legal. Why are we even here then? What did he mean by that?"

"It's probably just illegal to take orphans and turn them into assassins and stuff like that." Zed shrugs absentmindedly, moving on to his two large pieces of cold ribs. I sigh as I rub my temples in deep, circular motions. My eyes cast down to my worn tennis shoes, a migraine tugging at the backs of them. My lips pinch in a thin line, my eyebrows furrow. I don't know why I get like this sometimes, but I really do wonder why I'm even here in the first place, why I couldn't just stay a carefree orphan with no clear future, breaking into every piece of technology I see, why I couldn't just continue to be *free*. Assassin training is draining, physically and mentally, no matter what age you are. I never would've thought this would be my life.

At seven-fifteen dinner is over, and you either go to a class or hang out around headquarters until curfew, which is when you have to report to your dorm room at 9:00 and doors lock for the night. Zed has an encryption class for the next hour, but when I turn to hug and kiss him goodbye, he's already leaving the dining hall with James. I sigh and go to my dorm room to read. If only Zed would be here when I need him.

There are twenty apartment-style dorms here, and I get room number 20 all to myself. It's tucked in the very corner of the residence wing, all the way at the back of headquarters. I have a full size bed, a dresser drawer, and a mini TV, although it only has three channels. I have a closet with all of my old plain clothes, a desk, and a large window that overlooks the ever-bustling city. I have a mini fridge and microwave, and an old loveseat in the corner—my reading corner.

Suddenly, I hear something—someone is knocking on the window. At first I just ignore it, and continue to read my book about computers. Then I hear it again, more urgent this time. I groan as I put in my bookmark and walk over to the window. I freeze.

"D?" I say, opening the window just a bit. The sounds of the city and biting cold air instantly float into the room. "Y-You came back?"

"Of course, but I don't have much time." his gravelly voice whispers. Genesis is 20 storeys tall, with two underground levels beneath us. The Elite Training Program (ETP) operates on the first three floors and the dorms are on the first floor, so I suppose it was fairly easy for D to sneak to my room, if he cut the necessary security cameras. He lets his elbows rest on the metal bars that guard the outside of the window. If I lift the window any more, an alarm will go off.

"I can get you out of here," D begins. "but you have to do me a favor…"

"I-I never made a decision yet." I say, kneeling on the ground so our eyes are leveled. Well, I can't see D's eyes because of his hood. "Besides, I can't leave this place; they'll kill me if I escape. McCoy's already watching my every move."

"Not if you follow my plan." D states. "Look, if you want out, I can get you out now. But you need to make up your mind. *Tonight*."

I sigh. This man is my only shot at escaping this place. But there's only one person holding me back.

"Quit thinking about Zed." D snaps, as if he read my mind. "You said he doesn't even notice you half the time anymore. He's moved on from you, Skye. It's as simple as that. And now it's time for you to move on, for yourself. Or you'll be stuck in the same bubble for the rest of your life, watching him and all the others pass you by."

"It's not that," I say. "Zed's my best friend too. I can't just leave him after all he's done for me."

"He *was* a friend of yours, a long time ago, when you were kids. What has he ever done for you, Skye?" D asks. Even with his heavy hood on I can feel his cold stare on me. "*What?*"

"I…I don't know." I mumble. I can feel myself going weak, but I take a deep breath. I can't crumble now. I can't.

"What's your decision, then?" D presses. I gulp.

"…I'm getting out of here."

5

SATURDAY, DECEMBER 16, 2017
10:00 A.M.
CAMBRIDGE ESTATE

Harper

THE HOT CHOCOLATE IS cold now, but I give it to Jo anyway. She's wide awake when I return to my room, but is still weak. There are dark circles underneath her eyes, she's still overheated, and is still coughing up gross stuff. She sits up in my bed and takes the mug from me. 'Thank you,' she signs limply, taking big soothing gulps.

'I don't think we're safe here,' I sign before laying down next to her, wanting to go back to sleep and not wake up for a long, long time.

'Not safe how?' she signs after setting the mug down on the nightstand. She grabs her hearing aids off the nightstand and puts them on, yawning.

I decide to tell her everything, starting from when I woke up this morning. "I woke up about an hour ago and sat in the sunroom. I persuaded myself to think that the letter was just some stupid joke, but then…things started happening. First, I called Aunt Veronica to see if she knew anything. She said Mom cancelled all our holiday plans yesterday. And then…I think I heard a gunshot and people moving around, and her signal got cut off. I was about to run to her house to see if she was okay, but I found this notebook at our doorstep…" I motion to the yellow notebook sitting in front of us. Jo doesn't pick it up. "I caught the person who's been leaving the letters right before he disappeared, and he texted me. He *texted* me, G. He has *my* number. I asked him how he got it, he said connections, but I don't believe him…I don't believe any of this."

"What did he look like?" Jo asks, her voice airy.

"He was wearing all black. He had a hoodie pulled over his head. But I saw some of his face, though."

"What's his name?" Jo asks.

"He said to just call him D. You have to read the next letter, Jo. He's the only one besides Mom who knows about Dad. There's stuff in here about Mom too, and us…" My sister looks at me for a moment, then sighs as she picks up the notebook and flips to the first page. Without looking at her glass eye and the faded scar next to it, it's like I'm looking in a mirror.

While she reads, I text D again: Jo and I aren't safe here.

I know, is his response just a minute later.

Me: Can I call the police?

D: I told you that is acceptable, but they won't be any good to us.

Me: Won't be any good, how?

D: Scorpion knows how to cover their tracks and keep their crimes in the dark. All the police can do is put your parents on the missing list and do investigations. But you know you can't tell them about me and my letters—you'll have to hide them.

Me: I don't know if I'm calling the police yet, but I need help ASAP. My sister is sick again & needs to go to the hospital. I have to get her out of here.

D: Scorpion will most likely not come after you two, but I know someone that can help you get your parents back and put the rest of the ex-agents that are plotting against the Genesis Project in prison, before it's too late.

Me: Who?

When D doesn't respond, Jo drops the notebook. Her eyes look distant and far away. That means she's thinking. 'Mom and Dad aren't married?' she signs, but she isn't looking at me.

"It's okay, G…not all parents are together—that's the least of our worries." I say, putting an arm around her, but I can tell just by looking at her that she's hurt. Hurt because we're just now figuring out who our father was, hurt because something bad is going to happen to all of us, and we don't even know how we fit into this complicated puzzle.

"Who were you texting?" Jo asks.

"D. The one writing the letters. He says he's on our side, and he knows how to help us get Mom and Dad back."

"You trust him?" Jo says, finally looking at me again, but there's an edge in her tone.

I hesitate. "I don't, but I know I can. *We* can." Jo smiles sadly, and the room goes quiet. I can hear her wheezing. She leans on me.

"I have to get you to the hospital," I say. "But I don't know how."

"Ambulance?" Jo suggests.

I shake my head. "I don't know yet. I don't want to draw any attention to ourselves." Just then, my phone buzzes on my lap. D finally answered.

D: I can deliver another letter to you about the person who can help you, either tomorrow or Sunday. I was called to an emergency meeting at Scorpion's underground HQ. Do not text me until I text you first, I might change my number again.

I respond "OK" and turn my phone off, still unsure about everything.

* * *

The rest of the Saturday is quiet and uneventful. I sleep throughout most of the day, until an incongruous nightmare jolts me awake. I'm the only one in my room. The lights are off, so the room is eerie and dark with the little amount of winter sunlight. The digital clock blinks 6:34 p.m.

I groan as I sit up and stretch, a massive headache begging me to go back to sleep. But I can't sleep all day long when my sister and I are potentially in danger, and when an underground organization is ready to destroy my grandfather's agency after almost an entire decade of waiting.

I change into a pair of jeans and my favorite red leather jacket to at least make me feel like I'm awake and go into the hallway bathroom. I splash cold water on my face and stare at my reflection. My face is drained, dark circles forming underneath my eyes. It's no doubt I'm worrying myself to death, but I need to be strong—not only for myself, but for Jo, Mom, and Dad. There's a lot that I don't know, but I'm determined to learn everything I can, and hopefully D will continue to help me with that. Hopefully my gut is right, and I really can trust him.

I walk into the kitchen to see Jo cooking; the familiar smell of savory marinara sauce instantly fills my nose and makes my mouth water. I think she's cooking spaghetti. She wears a ballet-slipper-pink sweater under an overall dress. Typical Joanna clothes, old-lady like. I stand back and watch her cook. Jo is the cook of the house, not Mom or Dad, but Dad did get her started in cooking when we were about twelve years old, when his passion for cooking suddenly died. Before then Dad would cook 24/7, it seemed; cooking was his passion, and was the only time his mood wasn't sour.

When I was younger, maybe ten or eleven, I remember asking Dad why he wasn't a chef or owned his own restaurant or something. "My life is complicated, Harper," he said. "But maybe one day when things get better, perhaps we could open our own restaurant together." He said it simply and sadly, his accent carefully hidden in every word. I didn't quite get how my father's life was so hard; we had a big house, two big cars, plenty of food on the table, and him Mom were always smiling, at least when Jo and I were around. Dad got angry easily, but he was getting better at letting things go.

Now, I sit and watch Jo cook a perfect pot of spaghetti, just as Dad would. About a half hour later we're sitting at the dining room table, the pot in between us.

"We need drinks." Jo says, but doesn't get up from the table. I groan as I stand and walk to the fridge. It's twice my size and has one of those machines on the door that makes ice. I grab a liter of Sprite, two wine glasses from the cupboard, and sit back down.

"We're not allowed to use Mom's glasses," Jo scolds, but I shrug lazily.

"Mom's not here, is she?" I taunt. I'm tired and moody and just want to believe that this is all a bad dream, that I'll wake up and our parents will be here, sitting with us and urging us to talk about things like school and our social lives. Jo huffs and snatches the second glass away from me.

We eat in silence. Afterward, Jo stores the rest of the food for later and retreats to the den. I sit in the living room and turn on the television. The Channel 1 News is on for its usual six o'clock programming. Some weather lady is saying there's going to be heavy snow this Christmas, and I nearly forgot it's the holidays. But there's no Christmas music on the radio or bad caroling with Mom's sister or *The Polar Express*. I'd turned off all of the decorations and lights, so the house looks just as it would on any other normal day.

Below the weather lady, there's a blue strip at the bottom of the screen with headlines scrolling through it. *Two Armed Burglars Steal $11.3 Million in Jewels…Acre Wood School District Teachers Still Expecting a 5% Pay Raise…8 Local FBI Workers Confirmed Missing After 24 Hours…*

In a split second, I pause the TV. So the police *do* know what's going on. And they put Mom, Dad, Aunt Veronica, and five others on the missing list.

Are they investigating their offices? Will they come here?

Just then, the doorbell rings.

6

**SATURDAY, DECEMBER 16, 2017
8:11 P.M.
CAMBRIDGE ESTATE**

Harper

THE DOORBELL RINGS AGAIN, but at first I can't will myself to get up and answer the door. I turn off the TV and practically tiptoe into the foyer.

I look through the peephole, holding my breath. A policeman and a woman in a gray suit are standing at the door, their police car sitting in the driveway, red and blue lights flashing but silent. My hand reaches to open the front door, but jerks away as I remember. D said there are two crooked cops right in this town. What if they're *them*?

Plus, D said not to let anyone find his letters—I need to hide them. But I need to be quick; if I don't answer the door soon, the police might think something's up, and I'm definitely not about to let myself or D fall into any more potential danger, whether they're real cops or not.

I run upstairs to my bedroom, where the first letter and the notebook are on my bed. I grab them and go to my closet. It's a walk-in closet and half the size of my bedroom, and I always keep it tidy. A wicker hamper sits in the corner, and when I open it, it's filled to the brim with clothes. Perfect. I dig until I feel the cold straw bottom, set the letter and the notebook down, then let the pile of clothes fall back on top of them. I sigh in exasperated satisfaction. The letters are out of sight.

As I head back into the foyer, the doorbell rings again. I delete my conversation with D from my text history, saving "Unidentified ID" to my contacts. I take a few deep breaths before slowly opening the door.

"Good evening, miss. Is this the Cambridge residence?" the woman asks. I nod, a nervous lump forming in my throat, preventing me from speaking. The woman looks to be in her mid-forties, with frizzy black hair tucked into a bun, brown eyes, and a serious-looking face. I can tell she doesn't smile a lot. *KERRI WINTHROP, DETECTIVE* is engraved on her silver name tag. "I'm Detective Winthrop, and this is Officer Barlow. May we come in?" I nod again, stepping aside as they step into the foyer, and I close the door behind them. Jo appears, and sits down on the living room couch. I sit down next to her, and Detective Winthrop and Officer Barlow sit across from us.

"Identical twins, huh? Interesting." Officer Barlow says with a smile. He's younger than the detective, with spiky blond hair and a scruffy beard, hazel eyes, tanned skin even though it's winter in Pennsylvania, and muscular. He's dressed in the standard Acre Wood Police Department uniform, but it doesn't have any badges or awards on it. Jo and I don't smile back. We don't do anything. Jo takes my hand, and I let her lean on my shoulder.

The detective opens a small notepad to the first page and clicks her pen. "Are your parents Victoria Cambridge and Martin Eastman?" she asks, immediately getting started. We nod. "Alright. I'm going to ask you some questions, and you girls need to be a hundred percent honest with me. Understand?" We nod again. "Good. What are your names and ages?"

"Harper and Joanna Cambridge-Eastman." I say. "We're sixteen."

"Where do you attend school?"

"Montpellier Academy..." I reply. *What does this have to do with our parents?*

"Are you aware that your mother and father have been missing for 24 hours?"

"Our current evidence shows they haven't buzzed into their jobs Friday morning, so they probably went missing before then." the police officer adds.

"Well, what's the current evidence?" I ask. "Did you investigate or do anything yet?"

"We just investigated where your parents and family member Veronica Zane work. We would like to investigate your and Veronica's homes before we head back to the station." Detective Winthrop explains. "But first I'm going to finish asking the questions. Is that alright?"

"I guess." I reply.

"What were you doing on the morning of Friday, December 15, 2017?"

"I don't know. It was just like any other day, I guess."

"Has anything strange happened since your parents' disappearances?"

I hesitate, hoping nobody notices. I don't meet Detective Winthrop's eyes. The only thing that's strange is D and his letters, but I promised I wouldn't tell.

"Um…actually, nothing's been happening." I say. I feel Jo tense at my side, but she's smart enough to know I'm leaving D out of this. "We've been home the whole time."

"Alright, then." Detective Winthrop closes her notepad, and her and Officer Barlow stand from the couch. Officer Barlow takes over.

"We're going to do a quick sweep of your house." he says. As he says this, he and the detective retrieve white cloth gloves from their pockets along with small flashlights. Jo and I stay seated as they walk back to the foyer.

'What about D?' Jo signs when they're out of sight.

"It's okay, I hid all of his letters." I whisper back. "They won't find anything."

* * *

It takes Detective Winthrop and Police Officer Barlow approximately one hour to search the entire estate. They come back into the living room with blank faces.

"I'm afraid you'll have to come with us back to the station," Barlow announces, already preparing to leave.

"W-What?" I stammer, my heartbeat quickening with nerve. "Why?"

"There's nothing here that will help us with your parents' case," he continues. "The Acre Wood Police Department is a safer and better place to conduct business anyway. But don't worry, this shouldn't take long."

"There are plenty of things that will help us right here!" I snap. "Their cars, their laptops, their home offices—can't you use some of your special equipment and collect DNA or hair or *something*?"

"That's all back at the station," Winthrop says flatly. "Please come with us—"

"No." I say. Jo's frail arm links through mine, and she holds on tight. "We're staying. You can't make us go with you."

Officer Barlow sighs. He unhooks his walkie-talkie from his black leather belt and whispers into it with a low voice. "Barlow to Gold, we're switching to plan B."

"...Gold?" I whisper, so quiet nobody hears me.

...There are two crooked cops right here in Acre Wood working for Scorpion: John Earl & Antoine Gold...If they come to your house, do not let them in...

"Get some shoes," Barlow says, opening the front door. "backup will be here in two minutes. If you're not in the police car by then, we'll have no choice but to force you out of here." And at that, him and his "detective" leave. I watch them head back to their car, but they don't get in. I scurry to close the door and lock it, my hands trembling again, my chest tight.

"Jo, go to the den, *now*."

7

SATURDAY, DECEMBER 16, 2017
9:45 P.M.
GENESIS HQ

Skye

WHEN YOU'RE AN ASSASSIN like I am—well, *was*—training to be, the first thing they tell you is that you no longer exist. After you graduate training, you no longer have friends, acquaintances, allies. Everything is simply stripped away from you. You do what you're told, complete the mission you're assigned, and if you don't…let's just say you *really* won't exist.

Before I put my great escape plan into action, I decide to tell Zed goodbye. Although we've been childhood best friends and even staged a fake wedding when we were eight, as we grew older things just stopped working out, it seemed. It definitely didn't help when Genesis came and plucked us right from Brades that fateful day, telling Zed he was going to be a special agent, me an assassin. Well, I guess assassins don't get to love people. So saying goodbye to him shouldn't be hard; this was bound to happen sooner or later. I spot Zed in the large manicured courtyard, standing beside the concrete fountain in the middle of the lawn with Tillie, one of the girls in our group. They're talking and laughing, and awfully close. Suddenly, my chest tightens, and my mind backtracks. Suddenly, saying goodbye to Zed feels like a bad idea.

"*Skye, are you on?*" D's voice says in my ear. He got himself into the security cameras a few minutes ago, so now he can see the entire facility. D and his bulky computer are hiding in the bushes in a parking lot across Tenth Street. "Go to the main lobby, nobody's there. Hurry before guards arrive for night patrol."

"Okay." I reply, taking one last glance at Zed and Tillie before turning and heading back to the door, careful not to let my boots fall too deep into the fresh snow.

I have one frostbitten hand on the door before I hear him call my name. "*Skye*...? Skye, wait up!" But I don't acknowledge him. I yank open the door and step into the main hall. It's dim and dead-silent; curfew starts in five minutes. I need to hurry before all the doors lock for the night, and the laser beams turn on. I run down the hall to the main entrance, where Ms. McCoy had given me the manila folder earlier.

Beyond headquarters, the city is still alive and busy, the sky ink-black with no stars or moon in sight. I hear Zed's heavy footsteps catch up to me. I hear Tillie call, "*Zed*," with an annoyed tone, but she remains halfway down the hall.

"Skye, what are you doing?" Zed practically yells. My chest tightens. Time is running out.

"Be quiet! I'm going to get caught!" I hiss.

"Get *caught*? Doing what?"

I can't tell Zed that I'm escaping. That this place is full of lies, and we're not really important at all, that Genesis and the Elite Training Program are keeping things from us. I know it. And I don't want to be forced to be an assassin, I don't want to spend my life killing people. Before I realize it, I'm running out into the night. I see a bush shift in the distance, and I bolt across the eerily empty Tenth Street to it. I see a guard get out of her car, coffee in hand, scrolling through her cell phone. I look back to see Zed watching me blankly. I also see Tillie, whose arms are crossed, her eyes narrowed at me.

I duck down behind the bush, and there sits D, already packing up his equipment. He wears the same attire he always does, black jeans, hoodie, shoes. His hood covers half his face, as usual.

"All of the security cameras will unfreeze in three minutes. That gives us enough time to sneak back to my truck and get out of here." He motions to the rusted white pickup that sits right behind us. He glances past me, to where Zed still stands, looking around the parking lot like a lost puppy. Tillie is gone. The guard tries to urge Zed inside, but he doesn't budge. "Did that guard see you?" D asks.

"I don't think so, but we have to get out of the city, ASAP. Zed's probably going to tell on me any second now."

"Alright. On three, we army crawl to my truck. When I say so, slowly open the passenger door and get inside." D explains. "Don't slam it shut until I say. Okay?"

I nod. I peek out of the thick green bush to Genesis, which is two curved black glass buildings that blend in with the other modern structures, but is double their height. Zed and the guard are arguing, probably about my escape. But the guard doesn't seem to care. She shoves Zed back inside and closes the doors. I see Zed turn and dash in the direction of Chief's office, just as all the lights go out for the night.

"One…two…*three*." D whispers. We army crawl to either side of the truck. My jean jacket and jean pants get streaked with dirty snow, but I don't care. I'm nearly free. D opens his door, and I copy him. He puts his bag of hacking equipment in the backseat and retrieves his car key. He slides into the driver's seat and, after waiting a few seconds, motions for me to get in. I do, but I don't close the door yet. We fasten our seatbelts. D doesn't take his eyes off of headquarters. He starts the engine, and the sound seems a thousand times louder. I take a deep breath. "Close your door." D instructs, and we slam them shut in sync. The sound echoes. I know at least someone in headquarters heard it. D slams on the gas, and in seconds we're out of the parking lot and on Tenth Street, just a few feet away from a city exit tunnel.

An ear-splitting alarm sounds off in the distance.

* * *

"Where are we going?" I ask a few minutes later. My heart is fluttering wildly in my chest, my hands are clammy, and I'm beyond anxious. But I'm happy; I'm finally free.

Escaping was…easy.

Too easy.

"We're going to a motel a few miles outside the city. I know someone who can help us lay low while Genesis searches for you. Then you can do me my favor." D replies simply.

"I can't believe I trust you." I mutter.

8

SATURDAY, DECEMBER 16, 2017
9:45 P.M.
CAMBRIDGE ESTATE

Harper

INSTEAD OF GOING DOWN to the den, Jo follows me to my room. I grab my backpack, dump everything out of it, and fill it with things I think I'll need: cell phone, charger, medications, the keys to the Jeep, D's letters, $80 in allowance money. Jo copies me and goes down the hall to her room. She returns only moments later with her own backpack filled. "How much money do you have?" I ask her.

"A hundred twenty. Why? What are we doing?" I can hear the growing panic in Jo's voice. I put on a pair of good tennis shoes. I hear the sound of a vehicle pulling into the driveway. We're out of time.

"Get some tennis shoes and let's go." I whisper, although I know nobody can possibly hear us; our house is three thousand square feet of pure red brick. Jo nods and leaves. I take one last scan of my room to make sure I didn't forget anything, before I wait for Jo in the second-floor hallway. We then go to the den, and I close and lock the wooden door behind us.

The doorbell rings. The sound of it makes my heart clench.

"Dad said there's a bunker or panic room down here. It has to be somewhere…" I say anxiously, but before I start searching, Jo walks over to Dad's bookcase. He has six shelves of one-thousand-page novels, encyclopedias, atlases, and dictionaries, mostly about technology and coding and money. She lingers for a moment, then knocks the fourth row of books to the ground. And then I see it: a silver door.

"Jo!" I yelp. She startles, her hands flying to her chest. "You're a genius!" I add, and she relaxes, muttering under her breath.

Suddenly, someone knocks loudly on the front door, so loud I hear it all the way down here. "Open up!" Barlow booms.

"This must be the door to the panic room. But, how are we going to open it?" I say.

'Help' Jo signs sharply, pushing on the bookcase from behind. I sigh, but I don't argue. Dad will be pretty mad if he sees all his books are messed up—*if* he ever sees them again.

It takes a while to knock over the bookcase and move it over far enough to access the hidden door. I struggle to open it, the door looks like it's made of thick metal or steel, and I let Jo go in first.

There are no lights on and the air is stuffy, but I close the door and lock it behind us anyway. I use all of my strength to turn the lock because it's so heavy, and it secures with a firm *click*. Hopefully that means this is a quality lock, that we're safe.

I let out a breath I didn't realize I was holding, my body not shaking as much. Jo and I are safe.

I feel around the wall for a lightswitch. I find one and switch it on, but it's dusty. Gross. The panic room is the same size as my bedroom, so it's fairly big. All four walls are white and paneled, the floor gray concrete, and there is another door opposite of the one we just came through.

"Where does that door lead?" Jo asks warily.

"I don't know. Should we open it? Maybe there's a year's supply of food and stuff in there."

"Maybe…" Jo says, but she doesn't move. She takes deep, steady breaths, one hand grasping her side. She starts to speak, but before she can finish her sentence, she collapses.

* * *

I barely catch Jo before her head smacks off the concrete.

She fainted, another sign she needs help—and quick. I gently lay her down on the ground and take her backpack off her shoulders. I hope she put all of her medicines in here. I find her apple-red emergency inhaler and try to urge her awake, but she doesn't budge. I hear footsteps above us—lots of them. There's probably a whole bunch of fake cops searching the whole house for us now, but *why*? Why do they want me and Jo?

Then, as if on cue, my phone buzzes in my jacket pocket. I take it out and look at the notification. It's a text from D. Thank goodness.

D: I have the person who can help you get in touch with your parents and get you all to safety. We can all meet tomorrow night.

I hastily reply. There's poor cell service down here, but the message still manages to send.

Me: A crooked cop and a bunch of other people are in our house. Jo & I are in a panic room, but Jo fainted. I need to get her out of here before it's too late.

D responds two minutes later: I didn't think Scorpion would come after you, but don't worry, I'll think of a way to help. Just stay put, and whatever you do, don't open that door for anyone. You might be down there for awhile.

Me: How long?

D: If they don't find you tonight, they should give up. Scorpion is made of 25 men and 5 women. I wouldn't be surprised if they're all at your house now with a few staying behind to guard their headquarters. But don't worry, I'll come up with a plan: I'll call Scorpion HQ and say I spotted you two in the city or something, looking for your parents. Hopefully they'll all leave, and you can take the public bus to Smithson East Hospital.

Me: Are you sure that will work? I'm running out of time.

My heart sinks at D's response: No.

9

SATURDAY, DECEMBER 16, 2017
10:08 P.M.
UNIDENTIFIED LOCATION

Skye

D AND I ARRIVE in a small rural town outside the city, stopping at a place called the Starr Motel. It looks just like any other sketchy, run-down motel would; it has large neon signs that have lost their glow, a parking lot with nothing but potholes, the smell of cigarettes permeate the air, the once colorful exterior paint faded, most of the doors and windows are coated in bronze-colored rust.

"Swanee is a good friend of mine. She used to work for Genesis," D explains, killing the engine and hopping out of the truck. I follow him, although my gut feels off. We walk to the very first room that I guess is used to check people in and out. The room is tiny. One mustard-yellow wall holds fifty little gold keys. There are two sunken couches, a wooden front desk, and an old boxy TV that plays the news. A little gold bell like in all the old movies sits on the front desk, and D taps it in a sequence. Probably a code. Moments later, a woman appears.

"Good to see you again, D." the woman says. I wonder if anyone knows D's real name?

"Swanee, this is Skye." D introduces me to the woman, and I smile meekly. "Genesis called her 9."

"I can't believe they're still tagging orphans like that." Swanee says in disgust. She's tall, at least five-foot-nine. She has a short black bob, olive skin, muscular toned body, and a sharp, defined face with deep brown eyes. She wears a wrinkled red flannel and jeans with black boots, and she smells of cheap bar soap. An ugly scar lines the side of her neck. "Let me guess. Spy?" Swanee says to me, looking me up and down.

"They tried to train me to be an assassin." I shrug.

"Oh. You're under eighteen?"

"Sixteen."

"Hm. You look older. So that means you escaped HQ? How'd you do it?"

"Well, D just tapped into the security cameras and paused them. I just went through the front doors a few minutes before curfew." I explain. "It was a little too easy, but they knew I was gone when D and I left, anyway." Swanee nods.

"Sounds to me like their security is still garbage." she says before turning to D. "Don't worry, you two will be safe here." She snatches a key off of its hook and throws it to D, who catches it in a split second. Swanee grins. "You still have the best coordination, D."

"I know." D replies, but I can sense in his voice that he's smiling. He puts the key in his pocket. "You mind keeping Skye with you? I think she could use the company, especially from a woman and another former Number."

"Wait," I say. "Genesis recruited you too?"

"Not recruited. Taken, really. But I was in the Scorpion Project, not the Genesis Project—I was one of the only ones who didn't rebel, even though that dumb project took everything from me. One minute I was asleep in the Brades Orphanage, then next thing I know I'm being tied to a helicopter with nine other kids on our way to headquarters."

"I came from Brades too, but that's not what happened with my group." I say. "When I was eleven, a woman named Ms. McCoy came into my dorm room and said I was picked to train with them."

"Ms. McCoy is still there?" Swanee says, eyebrows raised.

"You know her?" I ask.

"Dude, she's like a million years old." Swanee opens the back door, and motions for me to follow her. I obey, and D nods to Swanee before heading to his motel room. Swanee closes the door and locks it behind us.

"McCoy told me she was the new president of the Elite Training Program when I first saw her." I say, taking in the room. "It's like she made the recruiting process less traumatizing, but the actual program worse."

The room is actually decent. There are two queen size beds with sleek black comforters and pillows, a silver dresser with a massive flat screen TV that barely fits on it, a fluorescent blue fish tank in the corner housing a school of yellow fish, and all kinds of modern gadgets and electronics are scattered throughout the room. The walls have been painted black. Large framed pictures of women on motorcycles line one wall. Video game consoles and CDs are piled in a corner. One bed is unmade, so I'm guessing that one is Swanee's. I sit on the neater one and take off my boots.

"One thing I learned from that place is how to go unnoticed," Swanee says, slipping out of her flannel and shoes. "that's how I stole all this stuff from the Best Buy at Acre Wood Mall."

"Wow…" I say, not bothering hiding the amazement in my voice as my eyes land on an unopened Macbook Air. Swanee throws on a worn T-shirt and turns on the television. "Go ahead," she says. "You can have it. Do you know how to take it off the system?"

"Of course." I say, already walking over to it. I sit down cross-legged on the floor, giddy with excitement, and begin unboxing it. Whenever I get my hands on technology I've never seen before, I can't help but get excited, like a little kid on Christmas Day. Just minutes later I'm hacking the system and removing the laptop from the grid, so no one, not even Genesis, can track it back to the Starr Motel or me.

"You're good at what you do." Swanee says, watching me from afar. "It's getting late, so I'm crashing for the night. If you're hungry there's food in the fridge, you can take whatever you want." But I'm too focused on the Google search I did of the Brades Orphanage to comprehend what Swanee said.

10

SATURDAY, DECEMBER 16, 2017
10:30 P.M.
CAMBRIDGE ESTATE

Harper

I TRY CALLING MOM'S cell phone. No answer. I try calling Dad and Aunt Veronica, but they don't pick up, either. Part of me doesn't expect them to.

There are footsteps above us. Scorpion is probably all over the place, searching for us. I hear their muffled voices and their heavy, dramatic steps. If they come down here and see the bookcase tipped over, they'll most likely see the panic room door. But hopefully they won't be able to open it. This whole place is bulletproof too…hopefully.

I check the time on my cell phone. 10:11 p.m. I yawn before shutting down my phone and shoving it into my pocket. It's still on full battery, but I want to be sure I'm saving its juice.

I look at the door opposite of the one Jo and I came in through. Maybe there's food and blankets and stuff in there? Jo could definitely use some cushioning. I stand and slowly walk over to the door. I reach out to open it, but there's no door handle. Instead there is a screen that's the size of my head, with a blue button and a speaker below it. I press the button without thinking, and it glows blue. "Good evening, Ms. Cambridge," a computerized, British-sounding male voice says. What the—? "All systems are updated and clear. What is your request?"

Four options pop up on the screen. *Lockdown On/Off, Call Genesis, Open Escape Door,* and *View All Cameras.* "Well, then," I mutter, tapping the fourth option. Twenty windows appear on the screen in rows of four, and I can see the entire house in green night vision, interior and exterior. Three customized black Suburbans sit in the driveway. Scorpion is all over the house and the backyard. They're rummaging through the living room, the kitchen, closets, bedrooms.

"Would you like to enable audio recording, Ms. Cambridge?" the computerized voice asks, and I nearly jump three feet. "My motion sensors think there may be intruders in your home. Would you like to activate the alarm system as well?"

My heart is racing again, my palms clammy, and I take deep breaths. "Y-Yes?" I say. Hopefully this thing doesn't realize I'm not my mother.

A few seconds later, I'm able to hear everything Scorpion is saying, but they're not talking as much as I'd like. Then the alarm goes off. It's high-pitched and so loud I can hear it all the way down here, without the audio. I watch as all of the people startle and begin to scramble. One guy pulls out a walkie-talkie and shouts into it, "*Abort! Abort to the trucks!*" and they all run out of the house. There are seven people in each car, a total of twenty-one people, and after a few moments, they all speed away, nearly knocking over a street light. *Is Scorpion really this stupid?* I think to myself. I look over all twenty cameras. The house is empty. I leave the View All Cameras tab before pressing the Home Lockdown On/Off button. Then, all the doors that Scorpion had left open suddenly shut and lock on their own, along with the windows.

"The house is currently on lockdown." the voice announces. "I suggest calling your father or Genesis's emergency services for further aid."

I clear my throat. "No." I say sternly.

"Okay, Ms. Cambridge. Would you like me to start up the jet and search for a route to safety?"

"The...*what?*"

"Your jet. All systems are clear for flying, although it is due for inspection."

I press the Open Escape Door button, but nothing happens. The voice says, "Please place your right hand on the screen for identity verification." An outline of a hand, most likely my mother's, pops up and blinks at me.

"This is crazy." I mutter to myself, but I place my hand on the blue screen anyway. Moments later it buzzes, and a green check mark replaces the hand.

"You are Harper Violet Cambridge." the voice says, somehow happily. "My apologies. You sound very much like Victoria. How may I assist you?"

"Yeah...isn't my last name Cambridge-Eastman?"

"My apologies, Miss Harper. Your birth certificate on my file says your last name is Cambridge."

"I...I don't understand."

"That's what your mother wrote on your and Joanna Lyra Cambridge's birth certificates. Your father, Martin Eastman, refused to have his name on the papers."

Ouch. Now I know how Jo felt earlier. "Well, what's *your* name?" I ask the voice.

"Victoria named me Bobby. I am here to help you and your sister in any situation and am programmed into all of your electronic devices." the voice—Bobby—replies, but it sounds like *Bubby* due to his accent.

"Wait, you're in *my* phone?"

"Yes. Go to your mobile's settings and scroll down to the bottom of the page. There will be a black icon underneath all of your other apps, with the title 'Bobby Services' beside it." I sigh as I pull out my iPhone, reboot it, and follow Bobby's instructions. Bobby Services is definitely here. I tap on it. How am I just now noticing all this? Suddenly the app opens, and the same four options along with a few extras and a virtual blue button pop up.

"I'm going to unlock the escape door and turn off this screen now, but you have equal access to me on your mobile, and so does Joanna." Bobby says, and I hear a faint click come from the knobless door, and the screen on the door goes black.

11

SUNDAY, DECEMBER 17, 2017
8:55 A.M.
UNIDENTIFIED LOCATION

Skye

THE NEXT MORNING, I awake to large strips of sunlight peeking through the window curtains and onto my face. I sit up in bed and rub my eyes groggily, brushing my hair out of my face. At first I forget where I am, and I look around frantically. Then I remember. I'd escaped last night. I am free.

Now what?

I have to do D a favor.

Then I will be 100% free.

What will I do with myself then?

I have no idea.

I don't know what kind of favor D wants me to do for him, but I hope it's nothing too major. I mean, what could he possibly want?

* * *

Last night, I did a Google search on the Brades Orphanage in Cape May, New Jersey. It doesn't exist.

It doesn't even show up on the maps. The spot of land where the building is supposed to be is nothing but grass and dirt. Did something happen to it in the last four years? If so, that would mean that the orphanage *did* exist at one point in time, and there would be a search result for it, or at least a news article or CNN video explaining what'd happened to it and the nuns and orphans it'd housed. So, no, the orphanage never existed.

Then, where did I spend those nine years of my life? Where was I really taken to when I was two? And Zed and the rest of us? Where did we *really* come from—?

Swanee comes into the room then, holding two styrofoam to-go boxes. The smell of cinnamon pervades the air. She turns on a lamp. Today she wears an orange flannel and sweatpants, her hair messy from sleep. "I see you're up. I made French toast."

"Thanks." I say, taking one of the boxes from her and opening it. "Hey, uh…can I ask you something?"

"Sure." Swanee says, sitting on her bed to eat her food.

"The Brades Orphanage was never real, was it?"

Swanee's lips purse into a thin line. "How'd you find out?"

"A simple Google search." I shrug.

"Hm. Well, I don't exactly know if the orphanage is real or not; the FBI could've easily taken it off the grid when they started the Scorpion project and the ETP." Swanee says.

"You're right. The place where the building is supposed to be is nothing but weeds and dirt, but they could have easily photoshopped it or tapped into the satellites' system." I say. "Also, on the day I was recruited…one of the guys who guarded Ms. McCoy said her revisions of the program aren't even legalized. Do you know what he meant by that?"

"He just said that to scare you. For some reason they don't want anyone outside of headquarters to know about the ETP, especially when McCoy came along."

"Oh." I finish off my French toast and throw the box away.

"D said he wants to meet you in the lobby in an hour." Swanee adds.

"Okay." I reply. "Is there a bathroom I could freshen up in? And possibly some extra clothes?"

"My bathroom is right here." Swanee motions to the door beside her bed with her half-eaten slice of French toast. "You can go through my closet for something that fits you."

"Perfect." I get up and head into the bathroom, which is just as tricked out and modern as Swanee's bedroom.

* * *

An hour later, D waits for me in the lobby of the Starr Motel. He wears his usual attire. I wear a white sweater, black skinny jeans and black Vans with beige soles that are a size too big. I smell like jasmine instead of sweat thanks to Swanee.

We step outside. The sky is a bright baby blue with no clouds and a tiny white sun, and most of the snow has melted. The area around us is dead silent. The only cars in the parking lot are D's white pickup and a cherry-red Harley Davidson motorcycle, most likely Swanee's.

"Are you sure it's safe to talk out here?" I say. The air is thin and chilly, and I cross my arms over my chest.

"Probably not, but Scorpion only comes to this town twice a month to trade. There's no reason for Genesis to come here." D scrolls through something on his cell phone—text messages. *Harper Cambridge*, the heading reads.

"Who's that?" I ask.

"The girl you're going to help. Her father and I were close growing up, but circumstances made us enemies," D explains. "Harper and her sister are in danger because of what Scorpion's about to do. Their lives may even be at risk…"

"Scorpion? You mean, the project that Genesis replaced?"

"Yes. They turned themselves into an illegal organization right in the city, but they're acting like a gang. They're getting into trading, mostly jewels and electronics and gadgets across the undergrounds of the east coast and the black market, but also weapons and guns and illegally printed money. They're trying to—well, they *will*—shut down the Genesis Project and get revenge on the ones who created it in just a few days. They're calling the process Operation Zero."

"And what does this Harper girl have to do with all this?"

"Harper and her twin sister Joanna don't know this yet, but their parents are lying to them. They're both fully involved in Scorpion and

Operation Zero; I saw them at the emergency meeting I attended yesterday. In fact, they were standing right next to me, plotting and playing with new weapons Boss brought in from Mexico. I can't believe their mother is going to betray her own father and abandon her own daughters…their father has been with Scorpion from the start…I need to get Harper and Jo to safety, *today*."

"Their grandfather is one of the main people who shut down Scorpion and created Genesis?" I clarify. D nods. "Their mother works for Genesis, and their father is a member of the new Scorpion?"

D nods again. "Their father and I have been members since we were teenagers. Their mother is just now deciding to follow his footsteps, for whatever reasons."

"And why do you want to save Harper and Joanna?" I question.

D clears his throat, looking down at his black boots, then up at the sky. "Because they don't deserve this. Just like my daughter, Dani." In a split second he tosses something—a little polaroid photograph—to me. With my quick reflexes thanks to years of training, I see it out of the corner of my eye and catch it with no problem. "She didn't deserve to be caught up in my mess," D continues. "Boss killed her right in front of me because she spoke her mind, and threatened to tell the police if he didn't let me quit Scorpion and clear my name…She was too young to understand…she didn't understand that with organizations like Scorpion, there's no escape. Once you join, take the oath, get the tattoo or mark, you're *theirs*…"

I look down at the polaroid. It's soft and yellowing, the edges worn. "She's beautiful," I whisper. The girl in the picture looks to be a bit younger than me, with olive skin instead of pale like D's, a square-shaped head like D's, long brunette hair, and piercing green eyes. She stands in front of a brick wall, looking straight into the camera. "I'm guessing she looked just like you."

"Yeah. She had her mother's eyes." D replies, thinking.

"I'm so sorry, D." I say, handing the polaroid back to him. "How can I help?"

12

SUNDAY, DECEMBER 17, 2017
9:00 A.M.
CAMBRIDGE ESTATE

Harper

I WAKE UP TO find out that it's morning. Jo is awake now, too. I help her take her usual morning medicines, and for a while we just sit, not doing anything. I don't know if D is going to help me or not. Frankly, I don't know much of anything right now. Everything feels so uncanny, like a realistic dream I can't wake up from.

"Do you know where that door leads?" Jo asks. We're sitting with our backs against the cold wall.

"A jet." I reply. Jo looks at me like she doesn't believe me. She rolls her eyes. "I'm serious." I add. "Let me see your phone." Jo hands me her cell phone. We have our thumbprints in each other's phones too, so I unlock Jo's phone in seconds. I go to Bobby Services and hand it back to her.

"What did you do to my phone?" Jo says, an edge in her voice.

"Nothing! Just tap a button, you'll see." She taps the Talk To Bobby button.

"Greetings, Jo." Bobby says cheerfully. Jo jumps with a shriek, her phone slipping out of her hand and onto her lap. "My name is Bobby. I am here to help you and your sister in any situation. What is your request?"

"Are you serious?" Jo hisses.

"Of course. Bobby and I had a whole conversation and everything while you were knocked out."

"It's quite alright." Bobby says. "Harper and I have become acquainted. I am merely a computerized voice with many functions and connections with the guidance of artificial intelligence."

"You say we have a jet," Jo begins. "Is that true?"

"Yes." Bobby says. "An Embraer Phenom 300. Your mother got it years ago from Genesis's warehouse. It is complete with a bedroom, bathroom, and a fridge and microwave, and can fly itself, but it isn't as big as you think. It's purpose is to fly you and your sister to safety and tend to your needs for long periods of time."

"Well, can we get on it and get out of here?" I ask. "Maybe we can stay in the jet until I know exactly what's going on."

"Of course. I am also programmed into the jet's system, so I can guide you to anywhere you'd like. But you need to get the key."

"Where's the key?" Jo asks.

"I can track down its chip by taking a 3D scan of the house…It's exact location is your parents' bedroom, somewhere to the right."

"Okay." I stand and grasp Jo's hand. I remember the house has been on lockdown all night; nobody's here but us. But I still need to keep my sister with me at all times. "We have to stay together, no matter what. Come on." She groans in protest, but I help her stand up anyway and we walk to the panic room door. I put my phone in my jacket pocket and Jo shoves hers into her overall's middle pocket. I open the door.

The house isn't as messy as I thought it would be from when Scorpion was here, and we head upstairs to our parents' bedroom suite. The door is wide open, a few drawers have been left open, the closet door broken off its hinges.

"I'll text D and tell him we have a plan to leave. He said he wants to meet us soon." I tell Jo as I start searching the right side of the room. Jo, however, sits on the edge of the bed and rubs her temples, sighing.

Our parents' bedroom is elegant and expensive. They have a king size bed with a comforter made of silk, with a pile of fluffy long pillows on top. The dresser drawer has tiny gold wire mannequins that display Mom's designer jewelry, but half of them are gone—stolen. The flat screen TV is gone too, along with Dad's box of intense workout equipment that I use to prep for hockey season.

I go to the nightstand on the right side of the bed and open it. The only thing that's in here is a small black box. I swipe it and open it. It's the key. The letters *EP* are carved into the black leather. Embraer Phenom. I take out my phone and text D.

Me: Can you still come over so we can discuss a plan? My mom has a small jet—an Embraer Phenom 300. We can definitely use that.

D answers about five minutes later: Embraer is one of the best private aircraft companies in the world. I can come today with Skye, she's the one who's going to help us. How about 4:00?

Me: Great. Is Skye a friend of yours or something?

D: She will explain herself when we arrive.

"I guess we don't have to stay in the panic room anymore, but I don't want you leaving my side, Jo. Okay?"

"I'm not dumb, Harper," Jo retorts. At that, she stands and walks down the hall to her bedroom, and closes the door behind her.

* * *

I copy Jo and take a much-needed nap in my bedroom. After only one night of sleeping on cold concrete, I've nearly forgotten how comfortable my own bed is. I'm happy to be under my warm, bulky blankets again. Before I know it, I'm in a deep sleep.

* * *

I stood with fourteen other children in a single-file line, including my twin sister. We all wore white T-shirts, black pants, and black tennis shoes, our hair tied back. The room we were in was vast and gray. Mom and Dad were at work just a floor above us. Jo and I were eight. The other kids were no older than eleven. We had just finished an obstacle course of some sort, along with a few written tests.

A tall woman with long black hair, pale skin, and circular glasses stood before us, writing swiftly on her white clipboard. She glanced at us every few seconds as she scrawled. A few minutes later she seemed to be finished, and held her clipboard at her side. She stood straight and formal-like.

"Only four of you have proved to me and Genesis that you are capable of participating in our newly revised Elite Training Program, and are well on your way to following in your parents' footsteps. I am very thrilled to work with you, and your parents will be pleased." the woman said. I didn't remember her name. "As for the rest of you…you are simply not good enough." I glanced over at my sister, who stood right next to me. She wasn't watching the woman like everyone else, she was too shy to make eye contact with anybody.

"When I call your name, please step forward." the woman continued. "Attica Scott." Attica stepped forward proudly. She was one of the few kids here who went to Montpellier Academy with Jo and me. Her parents worked with our parents here at the Genesis Spy Agency. "Attica, you are perfectly agile and cunning. You've completed the puzzles and mazes in the obstacle course in remarkable timing. When you made a mistake, you recovered quickly and got back in sync. Congratulations. Mr. and Mrs. Scott will no doubt be proud." Attica beamed. The woman called the other three names and praised them. "Paisley Cross…Franklin Lam…Cooper Grant…" They all stood beside the woman proudly. Then the woman called the rest of us and spoke to us one by one.

"Shawna Biggs: You took too long to get up and down the ladders that led to the box of keys. And when you finally got to the box of keys, it seemed you had forgotten the instructions and the advice you were given on how to decide which key would unlock the right door. Overall, you're slow, just like your father." Shawna didn't cry from the unpleasant report, instead stormed out of the room, saying her father would sue the agency. Attica and Paisley giggled at the outburst.

The woman said my sister's name next. "Joanna Cambridge." Jo still didn't look up. She could hear, she had her hearing aids in and turned on, but she was simply too shy to do anything.

"Jo, you're just like your mother. You let people take advantage of you. At the keys and door obstacle, you gave Shawna Biggs the correct key because you felt bad for her, and she advanced to the next obstacle without you. You let people pass you up as well. And halfway through the obstacle course, you decided to sit out because you were wheezing. You're too nice, too shy, and too ill. You're basically useless in the redesigned ETP." Jo's face scrunched up, but she didn't cry. She held it in. I, however, could instantly feel my blood boil. My hands curled into fists, and I bit my tongue. I took Jo's hand and walked out of the room, straight up to our mother's tiny office on the fourth floor. VICTORIA CAMBRIDGE, UNDERCOVER COP, *the sign on the door read in bold letters.*

But our mother wasn't there, and the office was empty.

* * *

I jolt awake to see Jo standing at my bedside, watching me.

"God, I hate it when you do that." I mutter, pushing the blankets off of myself and sitting up. My bedroom is colorfully lit by my lava lamp collection in one corner of the room, although my magenta and neon green ones are gone, my orange one cracked. The magenta one was my favorite. I sigh.

'I think they're here.' Jo signs quickly.

"Who's here? Mom and Dad?" I say. It takes a moment to figure out who she's talking about. "...What time is it?"

"Four forty-five."

"Ugh." I get out of bed and walk over to my full-length mirror that rests against the wall. It has a new crack in the top corner. My outfit isn't too wrinkled. Jo hasn't changed clothes, either. I go to my window and ever so slowly peek out the thin green curtains. There in the driveway stands a man in all black, and a girl with jet-black hair. An old white pickup truck sits in the driveway. I grab my phone from its charger on my nightstand and turn it on. I have one new notification, a text message.

20 minutes ago
Unknown Number: We're here. Sorry we're a little late.

"Come on. D's here." I say, and Jo follows me downstairs to the foyer. I cautiously unlock the front door and open it slowly. "Sorry we kept you out here. We were, uh, sleeping…Come in?" I say, but it sounds more like a question than a greeting.

"Thank you for trusting me, Harper," D says sincerely. His voice is low and gravelly, like he's smoked for decades. He and the girl step into the foyer, and I hurry to shut and lock the door. "This is Skye. She's going to help us."

"Help us with what? Getting my parents back?" I say as we all sit in the living room. Skye looks around in awe, as if she's never stepped foot into a suburban estate before. Well, not a lot of people have. She and D sit across from Jo and me, and she gazes at the large family portrait on the wall, which looks like it came out of the *Entrepreneur Weekly* magazine. She's pretty, with long raven-black hair, tons of freckles along her face and arms, blue eyes. D wears all black, his hood secure on his head.

"About your parents…" D says, rubbing his hands together. He sounds worried. "I don't think we can save them—I don't think they even need saving."

"W-What do you mean?" Jo asks. She sounds worried.

"You are familiar with Scorpion now?" D says. Jo and I nod. We both read his letters. "Well, I was at the emergency meeting yesterday, Boss needed to reanalyze some stuff, and…your parents were there. They're helping him make the final changes of Phase 1 in Operation Zero, like where they're going to attack the building, what data they're going to take, which security guards they're going to have to kill. Your father is testing dozens of guns fresh out the factory. Your mother is coming up with ways to force her father to surrender to Scorpion, and to give her his money. They're betraying the entire company and your grandfather in two weeks. They're lying to you—they've been lying this whole time."

I stop listening. D isn't making any sense. "That's impossible." I say angrily. "Our parents are *missing*. They've been missing for days. You must have confused them with someone else."

D takes out his cell phone and turns it on. He shows me a picture, sighing matter-of-factly. Skye looks down at her shoes.

Mom and Dad.

I snatch the phone from him, taking a closer look. Mom, Dad, and a few others are in a dim, brown paneled room. My father holds a large gun with both hands, smiling as he looks over it. My mother and another man are pointing at what looks to be a blueprint, talking. The man is looking at Mom fondly, as if he's proud of her.

"Who's *he*?" I say, pointing to the man standing next to my mother.

"Boss." D replies simply.

"And who's *Boss*?"

"Edward Bowser III. The first Edward Bowser created his own underground money-printing business, Scorpion, nearly seventy years ago. The notorious Bowser family has controlled it for the past three generations."

"This is…this is *fake*." I retort. "My parents would never be a part of something like this. I want to see them as soon as possible, they can explain what's really going on."

"Harper, let's—" D starts, but I don't bother listening to what he has to say anymore. I stand from the couch and storm off.

13

SUNDAY, DECEMBER 17, 2017
5:30 P.M.
CAMBRIDGE ESTATE

Harper

I'M SITTING IN THE sunroom again, thinking.

Can I still trust D? Are all the things he said about my parents really true? Are they really going to betray everyone like this? *Why?*

There's a creak in the wooden floor behind me, and I whip around in my seat. Skye stands in the doorway. "Sorry. Didn't mean to startle you." she says. "Can I come in?"

"I guess." I reply tiredly. She comes into the sunroom and sits in the chair across from me. "Who are you, really?"

She hesitates. "Skye...?"

"Why do you sound like you don't know your own name?"

"Well, since your grandfather is Chief, do you know about the Elite Training Program?"

"ETP?" I repeat. Skye nods. "I think I had a memory about it. Jo and I did some big obstacle course with a bunch of other kids, but only four were chosen to follow in their parents' footsteps or whatever."

"How old were you when that happened? Ever since Genesis hired a new president for the program, they do things a lot differently." Skye says.

"Jo and I were eight. How old are you?"

"Sixteen."

"Us too." I say.

"The ETP doesn't simply let their employees' kids run through obstacle courses and take tests anymore," Skye explains. "They're really top-secret now. Nobody outside headquarters knows about it, not even the government. I'm guessing you and Jo didn't pass?"

I shake my head. "No. But I guess I'm glad we didn't."

"I was an orphan named Delilah until I was eleven. They came to my orphanage and took me and nine others. They gave us numbers instead of names, mine was Nine. They began training us to become spies, assassins, undercover cops, special agents. It didn't matter if we weren't healthy enough, smart enough, strong enough. They forced us to get better, even if it meant using prototype medicines and drugs that haven't even reached the market yet, or pushing us to our limits all day every day. I never felt right in that place. I spent the past four years of my life training to become an assassin, but I didn't know what would happen to me after that. After you graduate from training, the outside world will still never know about you. You either die during your first mission or are always undercover. It's like you don't even exist. And I didn't want to spend my life killing people. So I escaped."

"So, you don't have a name?" I ask.

"They gave me a name—Skye—so I guess I'm going with that." she replies.

"Okay, then. Skye. I like that name—it suits you."

"I don't."

"Well, do you know why the ETP is doing those things?"

"I wish I knew. Look, I'm sorry about your parents, but D is telling the truth. Something is going on at Genesis, and Scorpion is going to destroy them. It's best if we get far away from here and get help—"

"What about D? Is *he* one of them, too?" I say.

"Scorpion thinks he's on their side, but he's actually been trying to escape from them for a while."

"I still want to see my parents. I don't know what's going on, but I still miss them regardless. Can't we just go spy on them or something? You know how to spy, right?"

"I don't know where Scorpion's headquarters are, but D does." Skye says. "I know he won't let us go over there, though, it's dangerous—they're one of the most feared underground organizations in the east coast."

I sigh. "I still don't know what I'm going to do about Jo. She needs to be hospitalized before something else happens to her, at least for one night. But without our parents, I don't know how that's going to happen."

"What's wrong with her?"

"When we were six, there was an explosion at Genesis, and Jo was one of the people caught in it. She got third degree burns on her head, everyone was certain she wasn't going to live. She was in the hospital for about three months. She got some kind of infection from the burns that spread to her right eye, and the doctors had to cut it out to save her, that's why she has a glass eye and some of the skin on her face is thin. Sadly, it's how everyone tells us apart now because we're so identical. But they didn't know that the infection had already spread more, and it wasn't just in her eye; it killed off most of the fibers in her right ear, which is why she can't hear loud sounds and her balance is off, she's a bit clumsy. After that, the only thing the doctors could do was put her on something like chemotherapy. Thankfully, it worked. But the chemo was too hard on her immune system, so ever since then, she's been kind of off."

"I read about the explosion in Genesis's archives…I'm so sorry, Harper. Things must be hard for her—for both of you."

"That's why I take care of her. Our parents are rarely home because they're always working—whatever their definition of "work" is. All we have is each other, and I don't want to lose her. I have to get her out of here. I can deal with my parents later, Jo is more important to me." I stand up. "Is D still in the living room?"

"Yeah." Skye stands up also.

"For now, we can all come up with a plan to leave town. D says Scorpion's next full attempt to destroy Genesis is on December 30. Hopefully I can figure out how to get in touch with my parents in two weeks." Skye follows me back into the living room, and we're all sitting down together again.

* * *

It only takes ten minutes to create a plan to leave town. It's fairly simple, and I write it down on a piece of notebook paper. Today is December 17, a Sunday. We plan to leave tomorrow or the next day.

1. Pack a week's supply (maybe two?) of food, water, clothes, etc. into the jet—basic survival stuff.
2. Go to Rite Aid to refill Jo's medicines & vitamins. Doesn't require a parent's signature, but will cost $200.
3. Have Bobby check the jet's systems and address any concerns.
4. Best takeoff time is 2:00 a.m.; when it's dark and Winchester is asleep.
5. Fly to ??

"Why did you write us letters instead of seeing us in person, anyway?" I ask D.

"I was scared to reveal my identity." D replies simply. "I delivered the first letter before I'd convinced Boss to pull me from Operation Zero."

"I kind of still don't know you're identity now…How did you get on my school's campus?"

"Same way I got Skye from Genesis: I paused the security cameras and tapped into the school's alarm systems."

"Where are we going to fly to?" Jo asks, but she sounds sleepy.

"That's what we still need to figure out." Skye answers.

"Why don't you get some rest, Jo?" I say, checking the time on my phone. 5:48 p.m. "Skye can stay here with you while D and I go to Rite Aid before it closes."

"Alright…"

"I can trust you, right?" I say to Skye.

"Of course." Skye helps Jo upstairs, and I toss D the keys to Mom's Jeep. "Ready?" I ask him. He nods. "Let's go."

***

Winchester is eerily quiet as D drives through the neighborhood. Most of the estates are dark and empty; most families are already out of town for the holidays, even the family farms are vacant. My classmates bragged about going to places like Mexico, the Bahamas, even Dubai. I'm pretty sure my parents can afford trips like that too, but we've never left the U.S. at all for anything, let alone Pennsylvania.

The sky is a scenic blend of pink of orange, the sun setting. I can already see a few stars. As we drive, I realize that all three neighborhoods of Acre Wood are quiet and empty, Winchester, Ravenwood, Belcourt. Ten minutes later we arrive in the Square, where there are plazas, restaurants, department stores, clubs and lounges. My friends and I go to Club 29, a lounge for older kids, when the adults hog the country club.

D parks in front of Rite Aid. It's bright on the inside, it doesn't close for another half hour, but there are no customers, just a guy behind the prescription desk. D sticks a wad of cash in my purse, and we go inside. I don't question where the money wad came from, it's probably from "Boss." D wanders off to the candy and gum aisle, and I head into the women's bathroom to count the money. I take the wad out of my purse and realize it's all fresh green hundred dollar bills. I slip three from the rubber band and look over the rest. This has to be at least a couple grand. I've never held this much money in my hands before…I don't think D would mind if I kept some…

I pretend to use the bathroom before going to the prescription desk. "Can I have refills for all my sister's prescriptions, please?" I ask the guy. He looks to be in his early twenties, with light brown eyes, acne on his cheeks, and a puffy afro. His eyes are half-closed with sleep, and he slouches tiredly.

"Last name and date of birth, please." the guy says, his voice monotone, pressing a button on his computer monitor's keyboard. I spell out our last name and give him our birthday, February 2, 2002. "And you want to refill *all* seven medications, including the multivitamins?" he asks. I nod. He sighs, pressing another button. He disappears behind the rows of prescriptions organized in alphabetical order. He comes back a few minutes later with a huge white bag with the Rite Aid logo on the side. He can barely hold it. "That will be $217.67." I place the three one hundred dollar bills on the counter. He looks at me quizzically, but hands the bag over to me.

"Keep the change." I tell him as I carry the bag out to the car, D following behind me.

* * *

At home, I put the Rite Aid bag in Jo's bedroom. Jo is fast asleep in her bed, and Skye is sitting in a bean bag chair in the corner, reading one of Jo's bulky books. I go into the living room to see D watching the news intently.

I go down to the den and stack all of Dad's books in one corner. The panic room door has been left open, and I go inside to get my and Jo's backpacks we hastily packed last night. The escape door is now unlocked. I push it open.

Past the escape door is like a small warehouse. The ceiling is low, but there are steep stairs that lead down to the floor that's now multiple feet below me. The floor is still bare concrete, the walls white, and there are rows and rows of things that I need to get a closer look at to fully see. The room seems to go on forever. This all must be under the two acres of land behind the estate.

And there, sitting just a few feet away from me, is the jet.

14

SUNDAY, DECEMBER 17, 2017
10:00 P.M.
CAMBRIDGE ESTATE

Harper

"WHAT WAS IT LIKE, being in the Program?" I ask Skye. We're sitting at the kitchen island, becoming acquainted. I guess we can be friends. D is asleep in the guest bedroom, Jo is still snoring in her bedroom, and I let Skye eat the rest of the spaghetti Jo had made. It seems like she hasn't had a decent meal in a while.

"If you didn't have any friends like me, than it was boring." Skye replies. "Every day was the same. Breakfast from seven to eight. Training from eight-thirty to noon, then a two-hour break. More training for an hour, then classes like calculus and language enrichment from three o'clock to six-thirty. Six-thirty to seven-fifteen was dinner, then elective classes if you have any that year. Then curfew at nine-thirty." she recites her entire schedule.

"I'm guessing you don't play any sports?"

"No. You?"

"Just ice hockey and tennis."

"What is regular school like?" Skye asks. "What's it like to be *normal?*"

"My family has never been close to normal—no family is completely normal." I say. "And Jo and I go to an academy, not public school."

"Are there school dances and bad lunches and drama, like on TV?" Skye asks, her blue eyes big with curiosity. For a second, I feel bad for her.

"Yeah. But the food at Montpellier is made by chefs, so it's good."

"Have you ever been to a school dance?"

"Just the Harvest dance, last year."

"Oh." Skye holds back a yawn as she finishes her food. It's getting late.

"D is in the main floor guest room, so you can have the last room upstairs." I tell Skye as she puts the plate in the sink. The house has five bedrooms.

"Actually, I'm going to take D's truck back to the motel we came from." she says, not looking at me.

"A motel? Why?" I ask, following her into the foyer. The house is warmer now ever since I turned up the heat, but is still dark with the little amount of lights I left on. All I see is the outline of Skye's face and hair, which shines blue because of the moonlight.

"Genesis is searching for me. Since your grandfather is Chief, he might send people here to ask about me before searching town, and probably even the entire state."

"There aren't any motels in Acre Wood," I say.

"There's one in the next town over, Northdale, but it's not on the maps. It's where people like me go to hide."

"What do you mean, people like you?"

But Skye sighs. "I'll see you tomorrow, Harper." She tries to open the door, but it's locked.

"Oh—sorry…" I unlock the door and let Skye out. She climbs into D's rusted white pickup and starts the engine. I barely see her in the darkness of the night.

"Do you even know how to drive?" I call out, but I don't think she hears me. But she does.

"I think I figured it out," Skye replies, her voice far away. She slowly backs out of the driveway, and in just seconds, she's gone. The last thing I hear are tires screeching on pavement.

* * *

The next day is Monday, December 18. I wake up feeling energized, and oddly prepared. I slept in until almost noon.

I find Jo in the kitchen, eating a plain waffle, a small bowl of fruit, and a glass of orange juice. New multivitamin gummies from the Rite Aid bag sit unopened. Her face is drained, pajamas wrinkled, hair tousled. She doesn't have her hearing aids on yet.

'Sleep well?' I sign as I open the fridge. There's not a lot of things in here. We're running out of food. I walk over to the pantry.

"No." Jo grumbles. I swipe a cereal bar from its pack in the pantry and go over to Jo. I hug her tightly for a few seconds, and her muscles relax. What can I do to help her, without the hospital's help?

I check the time on my phone. 11:52 a.m. I check to see if I have any notifications, but there are zero. Part of me wants to desperately call my parents, beg them to tell me everything. But the better part of me knows to wait, to get my sister and I to safety first. Who knows what Scorpion is up to this very minute—what Mom and Dad are supposedly up to this very minute. It was odd when Scorpion scrambled out of here two nights ago, and from the way D described them and their agendas, they couldn't possibly run away from the only opportunity to get me and Jo like that. That's probably part of their plan, to seem stupid under pressure when they're really not, or something like that.

We wash up and dress in similar comfortable clothes, leggings and flannels, and I tell Jo to bring her suitcase to my room, and to make sure her hearing aids are working. The first part of our plan is to pack a week's worth of stuff into the jet. We'll start with clothes. We don't need much, but we still need to be prepared.

'D and Skye coming with us?' Jo signs, letting her white suitcase fall on the ground beside my red one. She adjusts her hearing aids on each ear.

'They should. We need to learn everything we can about Genesis and our parents.' I reply, starting to pack.

'You trust Skye?' Jo asks.

'Of course I trust her. Hopefully she'll be back soon. I want us all on the jet by tonight so we can discuss where we're going to go.'

'Where did she go?'

I start to sign my response, but am cut off by the doorbell. The sound makes us freeze. Our doorbell is rarely used.

'Is Skye here?' Jo signs, but she doesn't get up. I practically tiptoe over to the window, and slowly peel back the curtain. A Suburban similar to Scorpion's sits in the driveway, but this one is gray. I can't see who's at the door, so I pull out my phone and go to Bobby Services.

I tap the speaker. "Bobby," I whisper into it. "Bring up any cameras that show the front yard, and zoom in on the best one."

"Would you like to see who is at the front door?" Bobby says. "There is a camera in the peephole."

"Yes, please," I say, my heartbeat quickening with worry. My cell phone screen then shows me an overhead view of the front door, and I nearly drop my phone, stunned.

"Jo—*look*." I whisper-shout. "It's Mom and Dad!"

15

MONDAY, DECEMBER 18, 2017
12:15 P.M.
CAMBRIDGE ESTATE

Harper

"WHAT?" JO EXCLAIMS, ALREADY standing beside me.

"Bobby, don't Mom and Dad have access to you too?" I ask Bobby. "Can't they just take the house off lockdown and come inside?"

"I'm afraid not, Miss Harper. I'm only programmed into your and Joanna's devices."

"But, you thought I was my mother when I first discovered the panic room. You listened to me then. Can't you listen to Mom now?"

"I only take Victoria's orders in emergency situations," Bobby explains. "I thought Victoria was in trouble. Otherwise, I was designed to help you and Joanna only."

I groan, snapping the curtain back in place.

Jo takes a closer look at my phone. "Wait…who's that man standing beside them?"

* * *

I turn off my phone and toss it into my suitcase, and Jo and I dash to the foyer. But D is already there. He's squinting through the peephole, both hands pressed against the front door, completely still.

"Uh…what's wrong?" I say, standing next to him. Jo lingers by the stairwell, one hand on the rail.

"We can't open the door." D whispers, not moving.

"Why? Those are our parents out there!"

"You don't understand!" he hisses. In my one whole day of personally knowing D, I can tell by his voice that he's scared for his life right now. "You see that man in the fur coat?" He moves over so I can look through the peephole, and I oblige. It's weird, seeing my parents just a few inches away from us after all of the turn of events, but they seem…different. A bad different. They wear black leather jackets and black pants. The man who stands behind them is a little taller than my father, who's six feet tall. He has medium brown skin, a shiny bald head, and wears expensive-looking sunglasses even though it's winter. A tiny white scar lines his bottom lip. He stands straight and tall in his black shirt, brown fur coat, white pants, and big suede shoes. A fat gold chain hangs from his neck. A cursive letter *S* dangles off the chain and rests on his stomach.

"Is that…?" I start, but I think I already know who it is.

D sighs. "Edward Bowser III—leader of the underground Scorpion. My boss."

I don't say anything else. I don't have the will to.

D was right, and I refused to listen. Mom and Dad are simply betraying Granddad and his company, Jo, me—our whole family. They were never really missing, they were with Scorpion this whole time. But *why*? Why are they doing this *now*?

"We have to hide." D says, looking around frantically. "If Boss finds out that I'm still trying to get out of Scorpion, he'll definitely kill me."

"W-What about Skye?" I hear myself asking.

"I texted her as soon as I saw Boss's car pull into the driveway. I told her to stay at the motel and don't go anywhere."

"She has a cell phone? Can I have her number?" I ask.

"She got all kinds of stuff from a friend of mine when we arrived at the motel last night. I'll give you her number after we hide." D says, looking through the peephole again. The doorbell rings again.

"*Harper? Joanna?*" It's Mom's voice. She sounds sweet and innocent—too sweet and innocent. Fake.

"H-How long have Mom and Dad been here?" Jo asks.

"Only a few minutes." D replies. "But they know you two are here. Boss doesn't know where I go outside of Scorpion affairs." D says.

"I know where we can hide." I say. "G, get your Rite Aid bag and go to the panic room, and make sure our backpacks are still there. I'll get our suitcases." I command, and Jo goes upstairs. I sigh. This is not part of the plan.

I grab our suitcases from my bedroom and take them down to the panic room, my stomach uneasy. D follows. I close and lock the door behind us, and the escape door is still ajar. I urge Jo and D to follow me down the multiple sets of stairs and to the jet. "Woah…" Jo gapes at everything. As we walk, I finally see what's on the long rows of steel shelves in the warehouse-like space. Boxes, dozens of them, all labeled. *Handguns, canned goods, bottled water, distress signals, earpieces, hacking chips, bullets.* Where did all this come from? Has this been here since Jo and I were born? Before then? What else is being kept from us?

Bobby's right, the jet isn't big (what did I expect underneath two acres in a suburb?), but it looks cozy. Just standing next to it makes my head spin; this is crazy, this whole weekend has been crazy. I pull out my phone and go to Bobby Services. "Bobby, unlock the jet."

"Okay, Miss Harper." Bobby replies. Moments later, all of the jet's lights turn on, and the oval-shaped door slides open vertically.

"Who's…*Bobby*?" D asks as we all climb the foldable ladder and step into the jet.

"He's a program," I explain as the door closes. "I'll show you later." Bobby is correct again, this is just like a fancy hotel room. "You know how to fly this thing, right?" I add, tossing him the key to the jet.

"Yes, my uncle was a pilot for years." D says, already discovering the cockpit. The room we entered has beige walls, small circular lights in the ceiling, soft beige carpeting. There's a black mini fridge and microwave with countertops in the corner, a black leather loveseat, and a flat screen TV bolted to the wall. The circular windows are tinted. There are two more doors to the left of the one we came in from leading to the bedroom and bathroom. I set the suitcases down on the ground with the backpacks and the Rite Aid bag. Jo collapses into the loveseat. She looks dazed. Then I realize she's crying.

I sit down beside my twin sister, but she looks away. My heart clenches. I don't like seeing her like this. "Jo, it's okay—"

"This *isn't* okay, Harper." Jo cries, her voice wobbling. "I want to see Mom and Dad. I want them to be here, with us."

"Jo, you have to listen to me." I tell her, taking her hands. "I want to see them too, but something's really wrong. I told myself that they were just missing, that none of this was really happening, but if I kept thinking that instead of getting answers, who knows where we would be right now. We have to face the truth, okay? We have to get out of here, just until we can figure out what's going on—"

The escape door slams shut with a loud *clash*. I peer out the window to see Skye.

She casually walks down to the jet, a black tote bag slung over one shoulder. I let her in, dumbfounded.

"What…? H-How did you…?" I stammer, but she only reveals a sly smile, her blue eyes dancing. Skye sets her bag down with the rest of the luggage. "Don't worry, I just drove D's truck to the intersection of Verdure Avenue and Ravenwood Lane, and parked it in the woods surrounding the neighborhood. I walked up a dirt path that led me to the back of this cul-de-sac and used my hacking chip to open the sunroom door. I figured you all were down here when I saw some guy in a fur coat and a couple in all black at your door."

I take out my phone again. The house is still on lockdown. I open all the security cameras and turn on the audio. Edward Bowser III and my parents are talking to one another. They sound angry.

"*I know they're in there.*" my father fumes, then adds in a lower voice, "*Do you think they know about the panic room? And the stuff your father gave them?*"

"*They can't.*" Mom says. "*They have no idea what their grandfather put down there to protect them. Besides, we haven't told them anything.*"

"*I can't be out in the open like this.*" Bowser says. "*Apparently my fake cop plan wasn't enough to fool them. I'll call some of my tech guys to get into the house's systems.*" I watch him pull out his phone and type swiftly into it. "*They'll be here in a few minutes. Let's wait in the car.*" And at that, he and my parents get back into the Suburban. My hands curl into infuriated fists. Why are my parents listening to *him*? Why are they doing this to us?

D reappears from the cockpit, anxious. "We have to leave right now. Once Boss's tech people get here, they can paralyze the jet's system and even the entire house, and we'll be trapped."

"So now how is this going to work? The whole town is going to see us take off." I say.

"Not all of Acre Wood," D says. "just half of Winchester. But I was taking a look at the cockpit and some of the jet's parts, and thankfully this thing is designed to be as silent as a mouse. Your parents and Edward will see us, yes, but once we take off, they won't be able to stop us."

"Alright." I take deep breaths to help clear my head so I can think clearly. This is happening. Right now.

Skye and I sit down on the ground next to Jo, and the three of us observe the security cameras on my phone. "Bobby," I call, my voice shaking. "assist the pilot during takeoff, please. We're getting out of here."

16

MONDAY, DECEMBER 18, 2017
12:30 P.M.
CAMBRIDGE ESTATE

Harper

D CLOSES THE DOOR to the cockpit. There's a window in the door's center, so I can just barely see him fasten his seatbelt, press a few buttons, and put on a bulky headset. I can just barely hear Bobby's voice, too, assisting him.

Suddenly, a massive bright light shines into the escape room and onto the jet, followed by a creaking sound—something's opening. When my eyes finally adjust, I see it. A rusted steel ramp has unfolded right onto the two acres of land behind our house. The jet rolls forward.

It accelerates faster and faster up the ramp, and my stomach flip-flops when we reach the sky. Out the window, I watch Edward Bowser III spring out of his car. Mom and Dad quickly follow. The last thing I see is them staring up at the sky in shock.

* * *

"We can go to a different agency or an FBI branch," Skye is saying. Jo had retreated to the bedroom as soon as D announced that we're on a steady, straight-line route. "A more remote one that's owned by the government instead of a single CEO."

"How many agencies like Genesis are in the U.S.?" I ask, messing with the tiny TV.

"Spy agencies? Not a lot." Skye stands and retrieves her cell phone from her tote bag. The icons and text font on the screen are slightly different. I realize she probably hacked into it somehow, so whoever's searching for her can't track her down. That would make sense. "Thanks to my four years' worth of elite assassin training, I can help us lay low. I'm pretty sure D knows how to hide out, too. The FBI branch that's the most disguised is in…" But her voice trails off.

"Where?" I say.

"…Cape May, New Jersey."

"Is something wrong with that place?"

"No…no, not at all. It's just…nevermind. I'll tell D to fly there."

"How long will it take?"

"We should be there in an hour or so. It's 12:45 now." Skye goes into the cockpit. Once I finally get the TV to work, I go over to the mini refrigerator and open it. It's practically overflowing with fancy drinks, cereal bars, bottled water, fruits, canned and boxed goods. I grab two skinny bottles of sparkling water and a few cereal bars, and head into the bedroom. Jo could definitely use something to drink. But before I can open the door, my phone buzzes in my pocket. I set the food down on the couch and take it out.

Mom: When did you find out about the jet?? Where are you going with it?

Mom: Please call me.

My heart clenches. I yearn to answer her, to tell her everything that's happened to me and Jo in the past forty-eight hours, because she's my *mother*, but I know I can't. Not until I find out the truth. The truth about her, Dad—everyone and everything. And until then, I cannot trust my own mother, nor talk to her, at all.

I grab the food and my hand grips the doorknob, so hard my knuckle turns from brown to white, and I breathe out through my nostrils, forcing my muscles to relax, before I open the door. The room is small, the beige queen size bed takes up almost all of the space, with a wide black dresser drawer, two black nightstands, a closet door in the corner, and a circle window. Jo sits on the edge of the bed, rubbing her eyes tiredly. I sit down next to her and put my arm around her. She doesn't push me away.

"We won't be flying for long," I say. "We're flying to an FBI branch in New Jersey."

But Jo doesn't respond. She's taken her hearing aids out, they're sitting on the nightstand along with some of her medicines. She slinks out of my reach and buries herself under the bulky covers.

I delete Mom's texts, throw my phone into my backpack, and collapse beside my sister, the soothing hum of the jet instantly putting me to sleep.

* * *

When I awake, the humming of the jet is ten times louder.

I sit up wearily. I stretch and leave the bedroom to find Skye sitting on the couch, fiddling with her fingers anxiously. "Skye, what's wrong?" I ask, sitting down next to her. "Are we getting ready to land?"

"Yeah. D found a strip to land on. He's lowering the jet in five minutes." she replies quickly.

"Great…Are you alright? Are you scared of flying or something?"

"No." she says, but she doesn't continue.

"Well, what is it, then?"

Skye sighs. "This…*this* is where I came from, an orphanage in Cape May. I was taken when I was eleven, but I found out that the orphanage never existed, at least not to the public. Whatever Genesis is doing with it, I want to find out. And I want to see if my birth parents are still alive and living there."

"Oh, I didn't know. I can help you. Since you're helping me and my sister, the least I can do is return the favor by helping you."

"Thank you, Harper, but I want to do this alone."

"Sure, if that's what you want." I say.

Skye finally meets my eyes. "I'm sorry—I didn't mean…You're nice and all, but I'm just used to being alone. Sorry if I sounded rude."

"It's okay. We've all been on edge lately." I reply. She gives a nervous, almost forced smile, and I smile back.

Suddenly, light turbulence sways us back and forth. Skye peers out the window. "I see the strip of asphalt. We're here." The jet gradually swoops downward, making my stomach flip-flop again, and I grip the side of the couch. Skye doesn't seem bothered. We keep going down and down, until the jet roughly scrapes the ground and slows to a stop, and everything goes quiet. A few moments later, D emerges from the cockpit.

"Well," he says. "we successfully made it to an FBI branch. The weather was clear, and we still have a full tank of fuel. All we have to do now is tell them our situation and ask to stay. But once we explain Scorpion's plan to destroy Genesis and transfer all of their classified information, they'll surely allow us to hide out here." D makes sure his hood is still secured over his head before walking over to the window and looking out of it. *One day I should just walk up to him and yank his hood right off his head*, I think to myself. *I'll see his face someday.* It looks like we landed in the middle of nowhere.

"Get Joanna and all of your things." D orders. "Skye, do you know how to get to the entrance of Branch 109? Do you have any Genesis ID?"

"Yeah." Skye stands and types something into her phone. "I can lead the way."

She grabs her tote bag and follows D out of the jet, and I go into the bedroom to wake up Jo. Thankfully she hasn't been moved from the turbulence nor the rocky landing. "Jo. Jo, wake up. We're here." Jo stirs. 'Did we land?' she signs, standing up. I reach to grab her hearing aids off of the nightstand for her, but one is gone. It must have fell during the landing. I look under the nightstand and under the bed, but it doesn't seem to be anywhere. "I'll come back for it later." I mutter before taking Jo's hand and leaving the bedroom. I grab our backpacks and put them on our backs, our suitcases at our sides, and we meet D and Skye a few feet away, pressing a button on my key to lock the jet. Hopefully nothing will happen to it, it's kind of out in the open.

"The entrance is 40 feet northwest. This way…" Skye says, using her phone as a GPS, holding it up to the sky.

We walk deeper into vast grasslands, the yellow grass and weeds getting taller until they touch our stomachs. There's no snow anywhere, but the air is still frigid. A few moments later, Skye halts. I look behind us to see that the jet is nowhere in sight.

"0 feet. We're here." she states, her voice merely a whisper. But, where's *here*? Then I see it. A metal square bunker sticks out of the ground like a sore thumb. Skye walks up to its chipping red door and knocks on it in a sequence—a code. The door has a rectangular view slit reminds me of what underground clubs have in movies, and it slides open in a split second, deep brown eyes staring back at us. The person on the other side doesn't say a word.

"FBI Branch 109?" Skye says, though she sounds uncertain, unconfident.

The menacing eyes flicker. "Who are you? How did you get here?" the voice hisses.

"We're from the Genesis Spy Agency," Skye adds, motioning to D, Jo, and me. "I'm from the Elite Training Program, too."

"You are? Then where's your mark?"

"Can't I just show you my ID card?"

"Sorry, miss. New protocol says I need to see your mark. It's the only thing that every ETP trainee has." The rest of us are huddling beside Skye, and I see her bite her bottom lip, her eyes averting down to the ground. Heavy winds blow above us, messing with Skye's long black hair. Jo shivers.

Skye mutters something I can't comprehend before turning around and lifting her white sweater to reveal her bare back. I squint to see a series of tiny typewriter numbers on the side of her back near her ribcage—her mark. The skin that possesses the numbers is dark red and slightly raised; like it's been burned into her skin and isn't supposed to be there, unlike a tattoo. I hope that's not the case. My heart sinks. What else is my grandfather's agency doing to people like Skye? Is this what Skye meant when she said Ms. McCoy only made the program worse?

011578

"011578." the voice reads to itself. "Hm. Alright. You can come in, but your little friends are getting checked at the next checkpoint." And at that, the eyes are gone, the view slit snapping shut. The door opens. Skye fixes her sweater hastily, her mood suddenly sour. Her face is expressionless, her eyes a dull blue and no longer sparkling, but I can tell by her body language that she is embarrassed. Is the mark bad? Did she not want anyone to see it for some reason? Did something happen to her to make her so uncomfortable about it? Was she simply embarrassed by the fact that this was the way she had to identify herself? This must be one of the reasons she escaped.

Skye leads us inside. D follows behind her, then Jo, then me. I hold Jo's hand and keep her close to me. We walk down steep dirty stairs, then down a long white hallway with bright lights in the ceiling and a white marble floor so clean we can see our hazed reflections in it. The hall is narrow, we can barely walk side by side. The person guarding the door is a skinny man with pale skin, a scruffy red beard, and large, jumpy eyes. He wears khaki pants and a black T-shirt with the FBI logo in the top corner. A walkie-talkie is clipped to his pants, an earpiece on his right ear. A gun sits deep in his back pocket, phone in the other.

When we reach the checkpoint, it's a huge door that looks like it would be used for a vault or safe. It's made of thick steel, and has a silver wheel in the middle, with a glowing green screen on the side. The man pushes past us and quickly types in the passcode. We hear two loud *clicks*, and the wheel spins into a blur until the door is about halfway open. "Your break isn't till two, Oscar," a voice on the other side calls, but the scrawny man—Oscar—enters anyway. The rest of us follow, and we bump into a tall man. He's pale with dark brown hair, in a beige uniform with all kinds of badges and accolades on his chest.

The inside reminds me of Genesis headquarters. On the outside, you would never know that an FBI branch operated here.

"Oscar," the man standing before us says. "Are you out of your mind? Who are these people?"

"One has a mark. I typed her numbers into the system, and it says she's an assassin-in-training from the Genesis Spy Agency. Genesis is one of our partners, right?" Oscar retrieves his phone and hands it to the man. I look at it as he does. A picture of Skye when she was younger is on the screen, followed by general information, date of birth, sex, height, weight, and some more code numbers followed by 011578. She doesn't look too happy in the picture.

"You." the man hands Oscar back his phone and points at me. "Who are you? And you better tell the truth."

"I'm Harper Cambridge, and this is my twin sister, Joanna. Our grandfather is the chief of Genesis." I say. "You know him?"

"Chief Ronaldo Cambridge?" the man pulls out his own phone and types something into it. "Oh, my apologies. I'm Chief John MacRyan of FBI Branch 109. Your grandfather and I are good friends. But, what are you doing here?"

"Have you noticed any changes in Genesis's day-to-day activities?" D speaks up. "Are they still in full contact with your branch?"

"No...?" the man replies, squinting at D. "Who are *you*?"

D takes off his hood without hesitation. I gasp.

"It's me, Chief."

* * *

"*Demetrius!*" Chief John MacRyan exclaims happily. *That's your name?* I think, but then I realize I've said it out loud.

"*That's* your name?" I say to D. "*Demetrius?*"

"Demetrius Xi, son of one of the greatest assassins who ever lived, Don Lee Xi." Chief MacRyan explains. He pulls D—Demetrius—into a bear hug, smiling wide. D's scrunched up face says he's not very fond of hugs. "Whatever happened to you! After your father died, you and your mother just disappeared. The FBI said you didn't have to go off the grid, you were safe. What are you doing now?"

"It's a long story," D says, trying unsuccessfully to get out of Chief's hug. "But now, we need your help. Something bad is going to happen to Genesis."

"What do you mean, something bad?" Chief MacRyan takes a step back, letting D out of his hug. His face grows serious. "Everyone to my office. Oscar, you're still on duty till two."

17

**TUESDAY, DECEMBER 19, 2017
11:53 P.M.
CLASSIFIED LOCATION**

Harper

ALTHOUGH JO AND I haven't stepped foot inside Genesis since we were kids, I still remember what it looks like. FBI Branch 109 has a similar setup, everything is just underground.

When you first enter, the main level is nothing but boring gray office cubicles and a cafeteria. But when you step inside the elevator that's tucked at the very end of the dark hallway, that all changes. The elevator is shiny and white and can hold at least twenty people. There are five underground levels that you can go to with a push of a gold button:

Main Level
U1: Training Rooms
U2: Weapons & Gadgets Center
U3: Residence Hall
U4: Technology & Vehicles Center
U5: Planning Center

Mr. MacRyan takes us down to the Planning Center, floor U5. When the elevator doors sluggishly open, I see an armed woman at the end of the long, wide hall. She wears a gray pantsuit and hat, black sunglasses hiding her eyes. The walls and ceiling are dark gray, the floor bare concrete, the lights above us dim. There are three doors on each side of us.

"This is where most of our plotting and meetings happen." Mr. MacRyan says, leading us to the last door on the right. He and the silent guard exchange nods, and he removes something from his neck—his ID card—and something on the doorknob scans it, a thin red laser going up and down the card twice. The door beeps, unlocked. "These walls are soundproof, bulletproof. Twelve inches of pure stone." Mr. MacRyan goes on as the five of us gather inside the vacant planning room. It's not very spacious, but can fit eight chairs on each side of the big glass table that sits in the middle of the room, with a dominant black leather chair up front. A massive flat screen TV is up on the wall, a few file cabinets and a water fountain sit in the corner. "Have a seat, everyone. Tell me, what brought all of you down here of all places?"

We sit. Jo and Skye sit on either side of me, and D sits across from us, hood back on. Mr. MacRyan caters us all small cups of water. "Thank you." I say gratefully, just now noticing how dry my throat was. Drinking the water makes me feel much better.

"Harper, do you want to tell Chief MacRyan everything that's happened to you so far?" D asks me.

"I-I guess…" I set my cup down on the table.

"If you don't feel comfortable talking right now, it's okay. Not many sixteen-year-olds are in situations like this—even the ones who have been in the spy agency business their whole lives. Chief, do you remember the Scorpion Project?" D says, all business now. "After it was shut down they attempted to bomb Genesis ten years ago?"

My heart clenches. That failed bombing was what nearly killed my sister. I turn to Jo. I notice her hands slightly tremble, her eyes averted to the floor. "Jo, can you hear me?" I question, placing my still hand on top of hers. She doesn't react. She can't hear me.

"Yes," Mr. MacRyan says slowly, sitting in the big leather chair before us. "Chief Cambridge told me the night after it happened. Said one of his granddaughters and a few employees had minor injuries…" He peers at Jo, remembering that she *is* the granddaughter who was burned along with four other Genesis agents.

"Jo's injuries were *not* minor." I say bitterly. "Do you know how much we've been through because of that day—how much *she's* had to do?"

Mr. MacRyan's eyebrows raise at my sudden temper change. "I apologize. And I'm sorry your sister is this way. My branch and other partners of Genesis have been trying to get better security there for years. I tried to persuade your grandfather not to build his company there, but he said Acre Wood was the perfect spot; your mother and aunt lives there, it's quiet, remote, middle and upper middle class, nothing bad ever happens there. But I told him looks are deceiving."

"We need to do something about this before it's too late." I mutter.

"After the failed bombing attempt ten years ago, Scorpion has been laying low, plotting, observing. Their next full attempt is in two weeks, on the night of December 30. Do you have files or records of them here?"

"I'm afraid not. Only Genesis and an FBI branch outside Pittsburgh have that stuff, and I'm not sure if they still have undercover cops and spies keeping an eye on their underground affairs. My branch isn't even close to Acre Wood, and I have my own problems to deal with. How do *you* know so much about Scorpion since the remaining agents rebelled?" Mr. MacRyan says to D, leaning forward, resting his elbows on the table.

D sighs. "I was...one of the ones who rebelled."

Mr. MacRyan's eyebrows raise again, his face growing suspicious. "*You*, Demetrius? With Scorpion? Why?"

"Well, they still think I'm a member, but they'll catch on that I'm still trying to leave very soon. Joanna and Harper's father and I Joined when we were sixteen."

"*Their* father? But, doesn't he work for Genesis with Chief Cambridge's daughter? He wasn't in the Scorpion Project or anything related to the FBI."

"It's a complicated story." D says. "But you do know what the so-called "underground" Scorpion is?"

"Yes."

"And you know their current motives?"

"I do not. But they're going to attempt to shut down the Genesis Project again…when?"

"December 30. Two weeks."

"So this is why you're all here? You want to stop the attack?" Mr. MacRyan questions. "There isn't much my branch can do."

"No. Harper and Jo need shelter and protection; Edward Bowser III is after them for whatever reason. And soon he'll realize that I'm still trying to get out of Scorpion, and will no doubt send someone to kill me, if he hasn't already. Skye escaped the Elite Training Program and is being searched for as we speak." D explains. "Can we lay low here? Just until we get things straightened out?"

"I see. I never liked the new version of the ETP…But, why aren't Harper and Joanna's parents protecting them? Unless…" Mr. MacRyan's eyes widen with realization.

"Our parents abandoned us for Scorpion, and I was completely oblivious." I say flatly. I might as well start believing the truth now. "They're fully involved with the plan to sabotage our grandfather and his new project, and Bowser tried to take us from our own house. He took our aunt Veronica, too…Wait. D, is she okay?"

D hesitates. "I haven't heard from her since the day they took her. I have no idea if she's dead or alive." he says. My heart sinks.

"Well, of course you can stay here! This is the perfect place to hide." Mr. MacRyan exclaims. "I just can't wrap my head around the fact that Martin and Victoria are Scorpion members—and you too, Demetrius."

"It's complicated, Chief. But thank you for letting us stay." D says sincerely.

"So, Miss Cambridge," Mr. MacRyan turns to me. "What happened?"

* * *

By the time I finish telling Chief John MacRyan everything that's happened, starting from when I got D's first letter, Jo is snoring, Skye is dozing off, and

D is…I can't tell. His hood is still covering half his face. Did I really take that long?

"Um, do you have the time, by any chance?" I ask.

Mr. MacRyan checks his phone and rubs his eyes tiredly. "Two-thirty. You can stay in the residence hall on the third floor, that's where most of my agents and employees live. We can talk more tomorrow afternoon, perhaps have a private meeting; I have a busy schedule right now."

"Sounds good." I stand, and everyone copies me in unison.

'What happened?' Jo signs.

'I told Mr. MacRyan everything. We're hiding here.' I reply.

The five of us take the elevator up two floors. When the elevator doors open, I see that the residence hall is elegant and warmer than the other floors. The walls are wallpaper, a red background with shiny gold flowers and green vines. The walls are framed in gold, the floor light brown carpeting. People are chatting and going from place to place idly, all wearing plain, simple clothing. We seem to be standing in the lobby area. There is a wide hallway to our left, to our right, and one right behind a front desk.

Chief John MacRyan steps in front of us as we take in the scene. "Luxury-style apartments are to your left. 1 through 10 are single bedrooms, 11 through 20 are two and three bedrooms. Lounges and places to get basic necessities are to your right, and straight ahead is the café, which serves everything from breakfast to dinner and is open 24/7. If you have any questions or if you need to reach me right away, ask any one of the agents on duty. Miriam," he turns to the woman at the front desk. "Please get my guests settled. I need to rest." Mr. MacRyan says and heads back to the elevator. In just a few seconds, he's gone.

"Would you like a three-bedroom suite? There's one left." Miriam says, typing on her computer. She wears a plain gray T-shirt and khakis, just like a few other people walking around.

"I think we all need to stay together." Skye speaks up. "You and Jo can take the first bedroom, and D and I can take the second and third."

"Perfect." I say. "We'll go with the three-bedroom."

"All right. You guys will be assigned to apartment twenty, the very last one. Do you each want a copy of the key?" Miriam says.

"Definitely." I say. Miriam gives us each a little gold key, the number *20* engraved in their centers. We turn left down the hall. It's much longer than I anticipated. Soon enough we reach the apartment. I unlock the door, and we all step inside. "Wow," I whisper. The sleek, modern apartment is complete with a kitchenette, living room, and four doors. One is open to reveal a grand bathroom.

Skye and D claim the rooms they want, and Jo and I go into the unpicked one, putting our backpacks and suitcases beside the dresser drawer. It's not until I've collapsed on the firm queen size bed when I realize how exhausted I am.

But tomorrow, I have work to do.

* * *

I wake up to total darkness.

Not remembering where I am or what had happened, I literally spring out of bed and look for a window to look out of. Then, yesterday's events start rolling in my head. *Jet…Escaping…FBI Branch 109…MacRyan…Underground…Hiding.* There are no windows underground. I stop, take a deep uneasy breath, and sit down on the edge of the bed. How long have I been asleep? Probably not long enough.

I search for light. I reach out to the nightstand and feel a lamp, and turn it on. A yellow glow illuminates most of the room. The room I'm in is modern and clean, the air cozy and warm. Two suitcases and two backpacks lean against the dresser drawer next to the the door. I hear snoring, and turn to see my twin sister fast asleep in the bed. Small beads of sweat coat her forehead. She's still sick. This place has to have some kind of medical clinic or a few doctors roaming around, right?

I find my phone and turn it on. It's on 81%, and I have a dozen new notifications. The time reads 7:36 a.m. I can get a few more hours of sleep before I look for Mr. MacRyan in the afternoon and tell him my plan. I scroll through all of my notifications before going back to sleep. Most of them are from apps and social media, four are texts from my mother, and one is a text from my best friend from school, Kat Daniels.

Kat • 1 day ago
hope your winter break is going well! :)
xander's parents are having a NYE's party @ the country club. ur going, right??

Once again, I forget it's the holidays. I sigh. There's no way I can tell Kat the reason why I'll most likely not make it home by New Year's…or ever. If the stealthy plan I've been thinking about goes wrong, who knows what will happen to me, and my sister? Who knows what Scorpion will do to us? And if my parents really are traitors, what will *they* do? I delete the text along with Mom's messages, and place my phone on the nightstand. I don't want to see what Mom has to say.

* * *

I wake up again three hours later, at eleven-thirty. I find Jo in the decent sized living room, watching TV and taking her medicines on the couch. "We have cable underground?" I ask, adjusting my light pink hoodie and leggings I'd changed into after showering.

"Apparently." Jo says, her voice hoarse. "But there's only four channels."

"We're supposed to be in hiding, so that's good enough. How are you feeling?" I ask, standing beside her.

"Better. I think I just had a bad cold or something."

"I hope so. I don't know if there's a medical clinic down here or somewhere you could've gone to if you kept getting worse."

"Where are you going?" Jo looks me up and down.

"Uh, just giving myself a tour of the branch." I lie. Jo can always tell when I'm lying versus telling the truth, but today she doesn't seem to pick up on anything. "We can all meet up with Chief later, maybe after we have dinner. Are D and Skye still here?"

"I don't know, their doors are closed."

"All right. I'm getting breakfast at the café. I'll be back later. Text me if anything's wrong." I make sure my phone is in my jacket pocket along with the apartment key before I leave. The halls are empty. I walk down to the café, and I'm the only one here. I scan the menu above my head. I order French toast and hashbrowns with orange juice, and wait at a tiny circular table for two. Just minutes later, a plate of steaming hot food is set in front of me.

"Do I need to pay you or something?" I say, but the waiter shakes his head.

"No one pays for anything here except for extra clothing and luxuries." And at that, the waiter disappears back into the kitchen.

I eat my late breakfast in slow savory. This is better than any food I'd ever eaten. Even Dad's cooking can't compare to this stuff.

I wonder if Dad will ever cook for me again.

SKYE

As soon as I awake, I bound into action.

As I wash up, I realize I didn't have any pajamas, that I wore the same clothes to bed. I can't get what I need looking and smelling like this; my hair is all over the place from being a wild sleeper, my sweater smells of light sweat, my jeans wrinkled. The time on my phone reads 6:22 a.m. I pocket the items I need and slip out of the apartment.

I stop at a clothing kiosk in the right wing of the residence hall, and ask for a new set of clothes. There are multiple kiosks and tables set up throughout the wing, selling all kinds of different things. There aren't many people here.

"Here." an elderly woman at the kiosk says. She hands me a sheet of laminated paper to read.

Items:
Long-sleeve Shirt — $15
Short-sleeve Shirt — $10
Long Pants — $25
Shorts — $10
Tank Top — $5
Tennis Shoes — $40

Sizes:
S through XXXL

Colors:
Gray
Dark Blue
Blue
White
Black

"I'll buy a dark blue tank top and black long pants. Medium size." I say.

"Cash or ID card?"

I hand her my Genesis ID card that's tucked in my back pocket. I see a table of small satchels in the corner of my eye. That can hold my personal belongings perfectly, without drawing too much attention to itself.

"What brings you to New Jersey at this time of year?" the woman asks, scanning my card before handing it back to me. About a year ago, I'd hacked into my Genesis ID card and transmitted money into it. I don't remember how much money I put on it, but apparently it's enough to get me new clothes from this place. Normally, agents just download money and information into their cards by a private bank or they have their Branch do it, but I like to do things differently. Clandestinely.

"Uh—apprenticeship?" I reply, praying this woman believes me.

"Oh, that's nice." the woman hands me a clear bag and my card.

"Thank you." I walk over to the kiosk with the satchels. They come in all different colors and sizes, and I pick the smallest one. I run my hands along its rough, cold surface. It's made of real brown leather. I purchase it and duck into the nearest bathroom.

I slide the new tank top over my head. It's a little too form-fitting for my liking, but it will have to do. The pants are perfect, and I've gotten used to my black Vans being a size too big. I finger-comb my hair and pull it into a low ponytail, and place my old sweater and jeans in the clear bag. I put the contents of my back pocket into my new satchel: cell phone, Genesis identification card, apartment key, hacking chip, flash drive. Being an ex-assassin-in-training and a successful sneak in an orphanage, I know how to get away with looking like I don't have anything.

I drop off the clear bag at the apartment, which is still dark and silent, and go to the elevator. I step inside and press the gold button: *U4: Technology & Vehicles Center*. Although it is only one floor above me, the single minute it takes to get to the fourth floor feels like it's in super slow motion. The more I think about what I'm about to do, the more anxious and jittery I feel. It feels as if a hand is gripping my heart and squeezing it, causing my lungs to constrict. I have to take deep breaths to keep myself steady, and force my mind to clear so I can pull this off flawlessly. I stand up straight, adjust my satchel at my side, and my training kicks into gear, along with the self-taught skills I'd sharpened before coming to Genesis.

The elevator doors open smoothly and silently, and I step out. The Technology and Vehicles Center is oddly empty and dim, despite it being six-thirty in the morning. When will the agents arrive for their work? I can easily tap into the system and read all the schedules to find out.

This floor is packed with all kinds of modern electronics and gadgets and vehicles, spanning out dozens of yards in every direction. To me, this is a heaven. I look around for any hint of security cameras. The walls and ceiling are pure gray stone, with no cracks or crevices for any type of device, the floor sparkling black granite. But there could easily be cameras, lasers, sensors, disguised in the metal desks, the Hummers, even beneath the floor. Either way, I need to be alert—and quick.

My eyes land upon an open door, and I step through it without thinking. The room has rows and rows of black keyboards accompanied by the largest computer monitors I've ever seen, much bigger than the ones at Genesis headquarters. I close the door behind me, and run to the very last computer. My body practically buzzes with exhilaration as I sit down and let my fingers touch the cool keys. I've never touched technology so...*new* before. With this kind of tech, I can do anything I'd like. The room has one rectangular window that gives me a perfect view of the elevator and some of the Center. If any agents come before I'm finished, I guess I can hide. But this should only take five minutes, maximum.

I tap the Enter button. The monitor's screen turns navy blue, followed by a white box with red text.

Hello, Agent K. Andrews.
Enter your ID number and password below.

ID: _____
Password: _____

I type the hacking sequence I know by heart, and the monitor beeps twice before it unlocks. I'm in.

I find the database for FBI Branch 109. Every single piece of information the Branch has ever obtained is right at my fingertips. I click on the search engine. My heart beats wildly in my chest as I type in the name:

Delilah Anne MacGabhann.

18

WEDNESDAY, DECEMBER 20, 2017
6:45 A.M.
CLASSIFIED LOCATION

SKYE

MY HANDS TREMBLE AS I retrieve my white 20-gigabyte flash drive from my satchel and plug it into the computer. I drag my file to the corner of the screen so I can look at both the search results and my flash drive.

The first result reads:

Niamh Anne MacGabhann: ID Card

I found exactly what I've been hoping for—and fearing. My birth mother.

The second search result is longer. If I click on it, a digital version of my own Genesis ID card will pop up:

Delilah A. MacGabhann — Genesis Spy Agency; Elite Training Program; Assassin (Daughter of Russia-America Embassy Agents Niamh MacGabhann & Erich Stanislav)

I click on my mother's name, and it brings up a digital version of her own identification card.

She looks just like me. Raven-black hair that's even longer than mine, pale skin, tons of freckles, muscular body, but her eyes are a regular dark brown. Her information isn't what I had expected. Born in Russia, has dual citizenship in the United States and Russia, works for the Russia-America

Embassy and FBI Branch 228 in Albany, New York, and…there's a death date in red below her date of birth. She's been dead for three weeks.

I copy and paste my mother's ID card into my flash drive as a PDF file. I go back to the search results page, unable to control my quivering bottom lip nor my glossy eyes, but I need to keep focused, I can think about my mother later. There are two results left. *Article: Beloved Embassy Agent Found Dead in Politician's Mansion* and *Erich D. Stanislav: ID Card*.

Just as I copy and paste my father's identification card, the elevator door opens.

* * *

My body freezes in shock for half a second. I force myself to remain calm and focused as I hurry to transfer the article and turn off the computer. I gently wiggle out my flash drive, stuff it into my satchel, and drop to the ground, getting out of the window's view. The chair squeaks under my shifting weight.

"*Who's there?*" a voice booms, echoing off the walls. I hold my breath as I scan the room for an exit. My well-trained ears hear heavy footsteps begin to walk, and I grow panicky. I spot a door opposite of the one I came in through, tall and white. It could lead somewhere, right?

I army crawl across the room to the door. I don't hear footsteps anymore. I reach up and grasp the silver doorknob. The door is unlocked. I open it just enough for my body to slide through, and the door shuts behind me with a faint *click*.

HARPER

I decide to wait to tell Mr. MacRyan about my plan. At the end of our meeting in the afternoon, I can pull him aside and hope he has time to talk to me privately.

I spend the day with Jo in the apartment. She seems to be getting better, no wheezing, coughing, blood, fainting. We watch TV, discover room service and order a basket of fries and fish sandwiches and sodas for lunch, and just relax. We do not let ourselves think about our parents and their possible betrayal. We do not let ourselves think about Scorpion, Edward Bowser III, our house, our lives in Acre Wood that we'll most likely have to leave behind forever—well, at least I'm not thinking about those things. I don't know what Jo's thinking.

I find a spare pair of hearing aids in Jo's backpack and help her put them on since one of the other pair is still missing. It's almost three o'clock, a good time to go find Chief John MacRyan.

I stand from the loveseat and knock on D's door. "Come in," a tired voice calls. I take one step into D's bedroom. He sits on the edge of the bed, slouched over his cell phone that lies his hands. His face is scrunched up, concentrating hard on whatever is on his phone. D isn't wearing his hood, I can see his face again. He wears a plain black T shirt with the same jeans and shoes. His hair is stringy and wet, most likely from a shower.

"What happened to your father?" I find myself asking. "MacRyan said he was an assassin—is that true?"

D glances at me from his phone. "Yes."

"Well, what happened to him?"

"He died just like a lot of other assassins did: a mission gone wrong."

"How come you aren't an assassin? Why'd you join Scorpion?" I press.

"A lot of people don't want to follow in their parents' footsteps, Harper. But I didn't want to be a part of something like Scorpion at first. I was simply in the wrong place at the wrong time…" D states, but he doesn't continue.

"What do you mean?"

"When your father and I were high schoolers in Acre Wood, we were wandering the city after a midnight concert. We got lost, and eventually ended up on the so-called "bad" side of the city. We heard arguing in an alleyway, so we stopped to see what was going on. That was our mistake. We walked right in on Edward Bowser III discussing an illegal gem trade with someone. It took a while for them to realize we were standing there, but when they did, I guess we'd heard too much. Martin saw the gems and guns being traded and threatened to call the police. He turned to run for the payphone, but Bowser's men grabbed us and kept us still. He told us that he'd be watching us from now on, that we couldn't tell anyone about what we just saw."

"How did he watch both you and my dad?" I say. "What's so bad about trading gems with people?"

"Some gems are okay here in the U.S., but it was the guns Edward was giving away that was bad; it's illegal to secretly give weapons to other countries. But Bowser wasn't kidding when he said he'd be watching. His men followed us everywhere since that night. They kept their distance, blended in, but Martin and I could still pick them out. When we would be at home with our families, they'd watch us from down the street. When we'd go to school, they'd watch us from the basketball court or just outside school property. They were everywhere. Eventually I gave in because I feared that my mother was in danger and I was mad at the FBI after my father died, and I joined. Martin simply joined because he felt he wasn't good enough for anything else; he had average grades, got a lot of detentions for stupid things like talking back to the teacher or smoking at dances."

"Then he met my mother?"

"Yes. Aren't we going to see MacRyan tonight?"

"Oh. Yeah, we are. That's what I came here to tell you. I guess I got sidetracked." D nods and grabs his hoodie from beside him. "Is Skye still here? Have you seen her?"

"I haven't seen her since last night." D replies. "Maybe she's still in her room?"

"I hope so. I want to hurry and find MacRyan just in case he forgot about our meeting." I say, walking over to Skye's bedroom. Her door is ajar, and I open it some more. The room is dark and empty.

"She's not here." I say. We're all in the living room now, ready to go.

"I'll give you her number so we can both try to reach her." D says.

"Okay." I say. I receive D's text message and put Skye's number in my contacts list, then I text her. Her phone number is longer and much different than an ordinary number.

hey, it's harper.

we're going to find macryan for our meeting. where r u?

I wait about five minutes for a response, but she never answers.

SKYE

"I thought you said the sensors detected something?" the voice says angrily. I can just barely hear it in here. I realize I've backed myself into a storage room or a janitor's closet of some kind. The room is no bigger than a tiny square closet, with a shelf lined with chemicals and cleaning products. It's getting hotter by the minute, and it's pitch black in here. I don't think I can sit in here much longer, but I don't have a choice.

"What did you say? Hold on, I'm on my way back up." the voice says, and moments later I hear the elevator doors open and close. Then everything is silent, the only sound I hear is my own shallow breathing.

HARPER

"I think we should go without her." I say.
"Where could she have gone?" Jo says.
"She has to be somewhere. Maybe Chief can find her in the security room when we see him." D says.
"Yeah, she couldn't have gone far." I add as we all leave the apartment. When we arrive at the elevator and step inside, I press the first button, *Main Level*. The ground beneath us shifts as we project upward.
"What are we going to talk to Mr. MacRyan about?" Jo asks me.

"I don't know exactly. Maybe a plan to stop Scorpion, and to see if we can get the other FBI branches and agencies in Pennsylvania involved. And hopefully we can find out if Aunt Veronica is okay." Jo nods, her eyes cast down. The elevator doors open, and the four of us step out.

"Where would MacRyan be...?" I ask myself, walking past the vault door we'd entered just hours ago, past the dull office cubicles where agents are busy typing and talking and analyzing, past the empty gray cafeteria. At the end of the main level is a door with a gold sign: CHIEF'S OFFICE.

I place my ear on the door to try to hear what's going on. Shuffling papers, ringing phones, and...Chief John MacRyan's voice. His voice is muffled, it sounds like he's on the phone. Should I knock? Should I wait? We have time. We have nearly fourteen days until Scorpion attacks, but who knows what they're really planning on doing. Before I can make a decision, the door opens, and Mr. MacRyan is standing before me.

"Good afternoon, Miss Cambridge." he says tiredly, exiting his office and closing the door behind him. He glances past me to see Jo and D. "What are you all doing up here?"

"Can we talk?" I say.

"About Scorpion's attack? No. There's nothing my branch can do about that situation. I've already called two FBI branches that are the closest to Pittsburgh and told them what's going on. I haven't told them about you hiding here."

"But, there has to be something we can do—something *I* can do. We can't just let this happen to my granddad's company. Not when we have so much time to take Scorpion down once and for all—"

"Look, if you want to save Genesis, you're going to have to go back to Pennsylvania and team up with their branches. I have my own problems to deal with—"

"*Mr. MacRyan!*" a woman in a white button-down shirt and short gray pencil skirt rushes up to Mr. MacRyan and hands him a paper. "There's been a change in the schedule. The boats will be at the docks tonight instead of this weekend."

MacRyan takes one look at the paper and grimaces, handing it back to the secretary. "The shipments aren't even close to being ready. Excuse me, Harper, but I have to go." He walks around us and disappears with the secretary.

"But, Mr. MacRyan, I…" I stammer, but he doesn't hear me.

"I think we should just let it go, Harper." Jo speaks up. "Mr. MacRyan is right; there's nothing he can do about Scorpion destroying Genesis. This is out of his power. Let's just focus on finding Skye."

"I agree." D adds. "Scorpion is a growing underground gang with deadly agendas, and they're quickly dominating the black market of the eastern United States. Not even I know what they're fully capable of. For now, let's just find Skye and take a day to think about what we want to do."

I sigh, a bit too dramatically. "Fine. But MacRyan's gone. How are we going to get to the security cameras to look around headquarters?"

"Just ask an agent." Jo shrugs. "Tell them Skye is missing and isn't answering her phone."

"Alright." I look around for any agents. The secretary Mr. MacRyan was just talking to is a few feet away, on her cell phone. "Come on." I urge Jo and D to walk with me over to the secretary.

I clear my throat. "Um, excuse me?" I say. The secretary glares at me with one raised manicured eyebrow. She's a bit shorter than me, with tanned skin, blue eyes, and surfer-blonde hair. "Could you help us?"

"If you want to see Mr. MacRyan, he's not available today." the secretary says bluntly.

"I don't think we need to see him," I say. "We need to get into the security room; our friend Skye is missing and she isn't answering her phone."

"I can't let you in Mr. MacRyan's office." the secretary replies. "That room is for authorized personnel only."

"We don't need to do anything serious, just take a look at the cameras." I say, getting annoyed. "Besides, we're MacRyan's guests, and this an emergency."

"Mr. MacRyan doesn't do guests. And I'm not letting you in his office." the secretary quips, and walks away.

"Now what?" I say.

"We don't need her to get into MacRyan's office." D states.

"What do you mean?" I ask, but he doesn't answer. He walks over to Mr. MacRyan's office door and kneels down on one knee. He wriggles something out of his hoodie sleeve—a bobby pin—and maneuvers it into the lock of the doorknob. He takes the bobby pin out and slides it back into his hoodie sleeve, and opens the door.

"We can't go in without an agent. We'll get in big trouble if MacRyan catches us in his office; he might even kick us out. Where will we go then?" I say.

"Well, let's hurry before he catches us." D says, stepping into the room. Jo follows.

"*Joanna.*" I whine.

"Come on, Harper. This may be our only chance to look for Skye." Jo calls from inside the office. I sigh and follow them inside, closing the door behind us.

19

WEDNESDAY, DECEMBER 20, 2017
3:18 P.M.
CLASSIFIED LOCATION

SKYE

EVERYTHING IS CLOSING IN around me.

I don't know how long I've been in here, but it's getting harder and harder to breathe. The air smells of chemicals. The Tech & Vehicles Center has been empty since I trapped myself in here; I haven't detected any footsteps, breathing, the elevator operating. Everything is silent, even my own hushed breathing.

Do Harper, Joanna, and D know I'm gone? Are they looking for me? Are they still resting in the apartment?

I wonder if they even care that I'm gone.

HARPER

The inside of Chief John MacRyan's office is modern and organized—so organized it looks like it's never been touched. The office is huge. There's a wide black-stained wooden desk in the center of the room, the wall behind his swivel chair lined with shelves and bookcases, file cabinets and an impressive fish tank sit on the opposite side, and a vending machine is in the corner. A massive computer monitor rests on the edge of MacRyan's desk with a white keyboard and wireless mouse. That *has* to be hosting the security feed.

D walks over to the vending machine, uses his bobby pin to screw with the money collector, and swipes a bottle of red Mountain Dew from the dispenser, still ice-cold. He opens it and guzzles it down.

"D!" I hiss. "Stop breaking into things! We need to find Skye and get out of here, *now*."

"Can I have a drink, too?" Jo asks D.

"No! MacRyan's definitely going to know something's not right when he comes back..." But Jo nor D seem to hear me. D steals a green Mountain Dew for Jo, and they enjoy their unlawful beverages together in the corner. I huff and sit down at MacRyan's fancy desk. In the corner of my eye are three picture frames, and I look at them. The first one is no doubt a young, twenty-something John MacRyan, posing in a blue Navy uniform with a few other people. The second one is of MacRyan getting married, carrying his beaming wife in his arms down the aisle. His wife is black, and they both wear Navy hats with their wedding attire. The third is of MacRyan, his wife, and four kids that all look the same, standing in what seems to be a park. His kids have light brown skin and curly auburn hair.

I turn my attention to the computer monitor. The security feed is already up on the screen, thirty cameras numbered and titled. I look at all of the screens over and over again, but I can't detect Skye's raven hair anywhere. I see a rewind button along with a few other buttons on the bottom left corner of the screen, and I click it.

I rewind to 6:00 a.m. today and double click on *Camera 15: Residence Hall*, biting my bottom lip in apprehension. The window enlarges to fill the entire monitor as a panoramic video. I can see everything, the café, the hallways, except for the inside of the apartments.

I begin to watch. At 6:22, I see a figure leave our apartment. Skye. I watch her as she goes to some kind of desk and get a bag of clothes. She then goes to another desk and gets a leather bag, and goes into a bathroom. I wait. Moments later she reemerges, this time wearing a tank top and leggings, her new bag at her side. She hurries into the elevator, and I hurry to switch to *Camera 2: Elevator*. Skye is still alone. She stops at level U4—the Technology & Vehicles Center—so I switch to the fourth camera to watch her there. She sits down at a computer, and I zoom in on her. She shakily retrieves a tiny object—a flash drive—out of her bag and puts it in the computer. She spends a few minutes clicking and reading before the elevator door opens. She scrambles to a nearby door and closes herself behind it. I fast-forward to the current time. She hasn't come out.

Where does that door lead? What was Skye doing? Is she okay? "Guys," I call. "I know where Skye is, she's on floor U4. We have to get there before MacRyan catches us." I go back to the main screen of the security footage, right where it was before I touched it, and stand up. D and Jo throw their now empty bottles in the shiny silver garbage can and follow me out of the office. "Thanks for the help," I mutter to myself as we walk to the elevator.

Luckily, we're the only ones in the elevator. We head down to floor U4, and I hurriedly walk to the door I saw Skye go through, Jo and D a few steps behind me. The red sign on the door reads "CAUTION: ORGANIC FUEL INGREDIENTS INSIDE. KEEP AT 100.7 DEGREES AT ALL TIMES." I open the door. It doesn't lead anywhere, it's a storage room. And there is Skye, sitting on the ground with her back against the wall, her skin concealed with sheen sweat. Her eyes are half-closed, dozing off.

"Skye, are you okay? Were you trapped in here?" I kneel down next to her and grasp her arm. She stirs.

"Harper…? W-What are you doing down here…? I…" Skye says, but trails off.

"It's okay, let's just get you out of here. D, help me." I say. D takes one of Skye's forearms and I grab her other arm. We help her stand up and get out of the tiny storage room.

"Will she be okay?" Jo asks softly, looking at Skye, who puts her arms around my and D's shoulders, breathing heavily.

"Hang in there, Skye. Hopefully MacRyan won't catch us now." I say.

"I'm alright…I just…my head hurts…" Skye says. We slowly head toward the elevator.

"When we get to the apartment—" D starts, but he doesn't finish his sentence. The elevator door suddenly opens. There stands Mr. MacRyan, four armed guards and his secretary at his sides.

"Stop right there!" he booms. We freeze.

"There! Get them!" MacRyan says, pointing to us. The guards rush toward us while MacRyan and his secretary take their time exiting the elevator. One guard prys Skye away from us and forces her arms behind her back. Skye winces in pain, her eyes squinting shut.

"Get off of her, she's hurt!" I say, although I know they don't care. The guard only tightens his grip. The other three guards surround Jo, D, and me.

"*You.*" MacRyan stands directly in front of Skye. "What were *you* doing in my database?"

"P-Please, Mr. MacRyan...I-I can explain...I was...I was just..." Skye tries to explain, but MacRyan shakes his head in disapproval.

"I got an alert from my phone saying a hack has been detected on floor U4. So I pulled up the security feed on my phone to see *you* hacking into a computer and transferring information from it. So I'm going to ask you again, what were you doing on my database?" MacRyan says, taking another step closer to Skye, his jaw clenched. But for some reason, Skye doesn't answer him. She lets her head hang. What was she transfering?

"Hm. I would send you right back to Genesis and let them deal with you, but Chief Cambridge and I are two very busy people. So I'm going to call Ms. McCoy to see what she wants to do with you. I also saw *you*," MacRyan points at me, "snooping around in my office. What were you three trying to do there?"

"*I* wasn't doing anything." I retort, feeling my blood begin to boil. "*I* was trying to look for Skye when your secretary refused to help us."

MacRyan scoffs. "That's no excuse. My office is for authorized personnel only—this entire facility is filled with things your eyes aren't supposed to see. In fact, I don't even know why I could trust you all enough to let you stay here. Demetrius, why are you hiding from Scorpion when they're not supposedly striking Genesis for another two weeks, and haven't shown their faces for over a decade? Why did your little friend here escape the ETP in the first place? Guards, take them to my office."

The guards grab us and force us into the elevator. MacRyan and his secretary walk over to the computer Skye was using. The elevator doors close silently in front of us, leaving us to stare back at our hazy reflections.

"Skye, what the heck were you thinking?" D hisses.

"I was just trying to find my birth mother." Skye admits, her voice wobbling with fear.

"*Why*? You were going to be an *assassin*, Skye! One time you disobey Genesis, one time you make a mistake and reveal your identity, and your birth mother is dead, along with the other people that are linked to you."

"She's been dead, D," Skye murmurs. "It doesn't matter what I do now, I'll never have the chance see her."

I take a shuddery breath. I look at Skye, but her hair purposely covers the side of her face. One of the guards still has both her arms wrenched behind her back, as if she's a criminal. The elevator doors open, and we are guided into MacRyan's office. "Sit." one of the guards demands. There are only two chairs in the room, and Jo and I sit in them. D and Skye sit on the floor in front of us. Two guards leave, and the other two stand in the corner, watching us. I can practically feel their cold stares from across the room.

About ten minutes later, Mr. MacRyan arrives. He sits down at his desk and clears his throat, resting his elbows on the desk. "I'm just going to cut to the chase: I'm kicking you all out. You have broken my trust and put classified information in danger. I already sent agents to your apartment to gather your belongings and bring them here." My heart sinks. Now where are we going to hide? Who is going to help us take down Scorpion? I know better than to argue with Chief John MacRyan, because he's somewhat right; I went into his office and on his computer, and Skye hacked into the database and stole information from it.

"I'm going to give Chief Cambridge a call." MacRyan continues, retrieving his silver cell phone from his pocket. He dials and waits. It goes to voicemail. He tries again. Still nothing. "Fine, then. I'll send him an email. You will all wait here until the agents arrive with your things, then you'll be driven fifty miles away from my branch. I'm deeply disappointed in you, Demetrius, and Chief Cambridge's granddaughters. I don't know what I was expecting in you, but this certainly isn't it…"

"Don't expect anything out of me or my sister." I say. "We may be Chief Cambridge's granddaughters, but we're not heirs to the family business—he never even let our mom train to be a CEO with her half sisters. Besides, we haven't seen our grandfather since the day of the bombing, and before then he never even wanted to meet us."

"Well," MacRyan shrugs apathetically. "your family problems aren't my problems, are they?"

I huff through my nose, my nostrils flaring, just like Jo does when she's mad or annoyed, and I stand, so sudden that the bottom of the chair screeches against the floor.

"We're not leaving with your agents," I say. "we have a jet. Where are our things?"

"They'll be here any second now." MacRyan looks at the time on his phone. Just then the door opens, and three agents wearing all gray are here with our luggage. I snatch my backpack and suitcase away from one of them. "Get your things, guys. We're leaving." I order before leaving the room.

* * *

Jo, D, and Skye meet me outside FBI Branch 109's bunker, luggage in hand.

"The sun is setting." D announces. "Does anyone remember where we parked the jet?"

"I remember when we got off the jet, the bunker was forty feet northwest." Skye says, turning around herself. "This way." She begins to trek through the high grass, and we follow her.

Thankfully, the jet is still right where we'd left it. We wait a few feet away from it while I retrieve the key.

D's phone vibrates in his back pocket. But before he can answer it, I hear rustling in the grass. Then gunshots.

Bang—bang—bang. Three bullets whizz past us and hit the jet's door, and three figures emerge from the grass, holding handguns. They wear bulky black pants, black T-shirts, black boots, and black beanies. One breaks the door with his gun and enters the jet. The other two grab Jo and take her inside too. I yell and try to run to her, but something—someone—holds me back. Two more men in all black appear, one has a grip on my upper arm, one is fighting Skye. I hear Jo's high-pitched, ear-splitting scream from inside the jet—the exact scream her self-defense coach told her to do if she ever got into trouble and couldn't hear. "*Jo!*" I scream, trying to get out of the man's hold, but it's no use. I wrench my arm the opposite way, and pain shoots up my arm and shoulder. "Let go of me!" I hiss, but I am thrown to the ground, which only hurts my arm even more.

"D! Let's go!" one of the men peers out the jet's door and yells to D, who's standing in the middle of it all, shocked-still.

"*Gold?* What's going on?" D says, hood off.

I look behind me to see Skye still fighting with one of the men. He punches her right in the face, and she falls. The man then grabs D and urges him into the jet, and D lets him take him. I realize that the jet is is slowly inching forward. I try to get up, but every time I move, an excruciating pain surges through my body. I cry out in despair; Jo is on the jet…

The jet is taking off. And all I can do is lay still in the grass and watch it leave.

Jo is gone.

D is gone, too.

I can only think of one plausible explanation: D betrayed me.

TO BE CONTINUED

About the Author

Bonnie Synclaire has been writing for as long as she can remember. *Rogue* is her first book, published at age 16. She also wrote several award-winning stories, one placing 3rd in the state of Pennsylvania in Reflections 2015. Besides writing, Bonnie enjoys dancing and reading. You can visit her at www.bonniesynclaire.com.